Great Britain Charity Commission

The Charitable Trusts Acts

1853 to 1894 - analytically arranged

Great Britain Charity Commission

The Charitable Trusts Acts
1853 to 1894 - analytically arranged

ISBN/EAN: 9783337369293

Printed in Europe, USA, Canada, Australia, Japan

Cover: Foto ©Andreas Hilbeck / pixelio.de

More available books at **www.hansebooks.com**

THE CHARITABLE TRUSTS ACTS,

1853 to 1894,

(ANALYTICALLY ARRANGED).

TABLE OF CONTENTS.

XI.—Amendments of Legal Procedure, and Creation of Summary Jurisdiction over Charities.

XII.—Provisions as to Repeals

APPENDIX No. 1.

APPENDIX No. 2.

MEMORANDUM.

The jurisdiction originally founded by the Charitable Trusts Act, 1853, has been gradually built up by the subsequent Charitable Trusts Acts, amending and expanding the provisions of the original Act. The original Charitable Trusts Act of 1853, and, consequently, the subsequent Acts, are concerned with various and distinct incidents of jurisdiction which are in some degree or other treated separately in the Acts, with the result that nearly every Act is both multifarious and at the same time incomplete in itself.

Of this condition of the Charitable Trusts Acts proof is furnished by the numerous cross references appended to the recent collective edition of the Charitable Trusts Acts, as well as by similar references appended to those Acts, as comprised in the 3rd edition of Tudor's Law of Charitable Trusts, pp. 466-566.

The following pages are the result of an attempt to dispense with the laborious and somewhat hazardous process of cross reference by bringing together, as closely as may be, the several provisions of the Acts, which deal with the same heads of jurisdiction.

The analysis of the Acts, upon which this arrangement of their provisions is based, is to be found in Table A. in Appendix 12 to the Report of the Select Committee of the House of Commons, which was appointed in 1894 to inquire " whether it is desirable " to take measures to bring the action of the Charity Commission " more directly under the control of Parliament, and to give it more " effectual means of dealing with the business which will come " before it."

The entire text of the several Charitable Trusts Acts, 1853-1894, is reproduced verbatim in the following pages. In a few cases, and conspicuously in those of sections 2, 4, 6, and 8 of the Charitable Trusts Act, 1860, it has been found convenient, in order to avoid confusion and repetition, to break up sections which deal with more than one of the several heads of analysis. In these cases, whenever the section thus divided is not to be found complete in any other place in the text, it is printed in full in Appendix, No. 1, for purposes of reference.

No attempt to consolidate has been made, and each section is treated independently. Some difficulty has consequently been experienced in determining the order in which sections falling under the same head shall be arranged, so as to present the state of the law as clearly as may be. In order to meet this difficulty chronological sequence has been disregarded in several cases.

In a few cases, pp. 8, 15, 22, 31, 63, and 66, it has been found necessary to completeness to introduce sections of Acts other than the Charitable Trusts Acts.

It is believed that the analytical arrangement of the Charitable Trusts Acts which has been thus undertaken may be of use to those who, not being fully conversant with the complexities of the Acts, desire to consult them literally for a particular purpose, and, further, that it may furnish a step towards a future consolidation of the Charitable Trusts Acts, whenever such a measure may be deemed to be practicable.

August 1896.

ANALYTICAL ARRANGEMENT

OF

THE CHARITABLE TRUSTS ACTS, 1853 TO 1894.

NOTE.—Any section or portion of a section of the Charitable Trusts Acts, 1853 to 1894, which is now repealed, or for which any other provision is expressly made by a subsequent Act, is printed in italics.

The following abbreviations are used, viz.:—

C. T. Act, 1853, indicates The Charitable Trusts Act, 1853, 16 & 17 Vict. c. 137.

C. T. Act, 1855, indicates The Charitable Trusts Amendment Act, 1855, 18 & 19 Vict. c. 124.

C. T. Act, 1860, indicates The Charitable Trusts Act, 1860, 23 & 24 Vict. c. 136.

C. T. Act, 1862, indicates The Charitable Trusts Act, 1862, 25 & 26 Vict. c. 112.

C. T. Act, 1869, indicates The Charitable Trusts Act, 1869, 32 & 33 Vict. c. 110.

C. T. Act, 1887, indicates The Charitable Trusts Act, 1887, 50 & 51 Vict. c. 49.

C. T. Act, 1891, indicates The Charitable Trusts (Recovery) Act, 1891, 54 Vict. c. 17.

C. T. Act, 1894, indicates The Charitable Trusts (Places of Religious Worship) Amendment Act, 1894, 57 & 58 Vict. c. 35.

I.—Provisions as to Short Titles, Construction and Extent of Acts, Interpretation of Terms, &c.

(a.) SHORT TITLES AND CONSTRUCTION.

[C. T. Act, 1853.] 68. This Act may be cited as "The Charitable Trusts Act, 1853." *Short Title.*

[C. T. Act, 1855.] 50. This Act may be cited as "The Charitable Trusts Amendment Act, 1855." *Short Title.*

[C. T. Act, 1855.] 1. "The Charitable Trusts Act, 1853," hereinafter called "the principal Act," and this Act, shall be construed together as One Act, and any Provisions of the principal Act inconsistent with this Act are hereby repealed. *16 & 17 Vict. c. 137. and this Act to be construed together.*

Short Title.

[**C. T. Act, 1860.**] 25. This Act may be cited for all Purposes by the Short Title of "The Charitable Trusts Act, 1860."

The Charitable Trusts Acts to be construed with this Act.

[**C. T. Act, 1860.**] 1. "The Charitable Trusts Act, 1853," and "The Charitable Trusts Amendment Act, 1855," and this Act, shall be construed together as One Act, and any Provisions of the said former Acts inconsistent with this Act are hereby repealed.

Short title.

[**C. T. Act, 1869.**] 1. This Act may be cited as "The Charitable Trusts Act, 1869."

Act to be construed with 16 & 17 Vict. c. 137. 18 & 19 Vict. c. 124. 23 & 24 Vict. c. 136. 25 & 26 Vict. c. 112.

[**C. T. Act, 1869.**] 3. This Act, so far as is consistent with the tenor thereof, shall be construed as one with the Charitable Trusts Act, 1853, the Charitable Trusts Amendment Act, 1855, and the Charitable Trusts Act, 1860, and the *Act of the session of the twenty-fifth and twenty-sixth years of the reign of Her present Majesty, chapter one hundred and twelve, "for "establishing the jurisdiction of the Charity Commissioners in certain cases" (which may be cited as the* Charitable Trusts Act, 1862), *and those Acts, together with this Act, may be cited as the Charitable Trusts Acts, 1853 to 1869.*

Short title.

[**C. T. Act, 1887.**] 1. This Act may be cited as the Charitable Trusts Act, 1887, and shall be construed as one with the Charitable Trusts Acts, 1853 to 1869, and, together with those Acts, may be cited as the Charitable Trusts Acts, 1853 to 1887.

Short title and construction.

[**C. T. Act, 1891.**] 1. This Act, so far as is consistent with the tenor thereof, shall be construed together with the Charitable Trusts Acts, 1853 to 1869, and those Acts and this Act may be cited together as the Charitable Trusts Acts, 1853 to 1891, and this Act may be cited as the Charitable Trusts (Recovery) Act, 1891.

Short title.

[**C. T. Act, 1894.**] 1. This Act may be cited as the Charitable Trusts (Places of Religious Worship) Amendment Act, 1894.

Construction.

[**C. T. Act, 1894.**] 3. This Act, so far as consistent with the tenor thereof, shall be construed as one with the Charitable Trusts Acts, 1853 to 1891, and with the Places of Worship Registration Act, 1855, and this Act and the Charitable Trusts Acts, 1853 to 1891, may be cited as the Charitable Trusts Acts, 1853 to 1894.

Citation of Acts in Schedule.

[**Short Titles Act, 1896, (59 & 60 Vict. c. 14)**] 1. Each of the Acts mentioned in the First Schedule to this Act may, without prejudice to any other mode of citation, be cited by the short title therein mentioned in that behalf.

Collective titles.

2.—(1.) Each of the groups of Acts mentioned in the Second Schedule to this Act may, without prejudice to any other mode of citation, be cited by the collective title therein mentioned in that behalf.

(2.) If it is provided that any Act passed after this Act may, as to the whole or any part thereof, be cited with any of the groups of Acts mentioned in the Second Schedule to this Act, or with any group of Acts to which a collective title has been given by any Act passed before this Act, that group shall be construed as including that Act or part, and, if the collective title of the group states the first and last years of the group, the year in which that Act is passed shall be substituted for the last year of the group, and so on as often as a subsequent Act or part is added to the group.

[* *Repealed by the Statute Law Revision (No. 2) Act, 1893 (56 & 57 Vict. c. 54.). In the repealing Act, the section is by mistake referred to as section 2.*]

SCHEDULES.

FIRST SCHEDULE.
SHORT TITLES.

Session and Chapter.		Title.	Short Title.
.	.	.	.
25 & 26 Vict. c. 112.	-	An Act for establishing the Jurisdiction of the Charity Commissioners in certain cases.	The Charitable Trusts Act, 1862.
.	.	.	.

SECOND SCHEDULE.
COLLECTIVE TITLES.

Session and Chapter.		Short Title.	Collective Title.
.	.	.	.
16 & 17 Vict. c. 137.	-	The Charitable Trusts Act, 1853 -	
18 & 19 Vict. c. 124.	-	The Charitable Trusts Amendment Act, 1855.	
23 & 24 Vict. c. 136.	-	The Charitable Trusts Act, 1860 -	
25 & 26 Vict. c. 112.	-	The Charitable Trusts Act, 1862 -	The Charitable Trusts Acts, 1853 to 1894.
32 & 33 Vict. c. 110.	-	The Charitable Trusts Act, 1869 -	
50 & 51 Vict. c. 49.	-	The Charitable Trusts Act, 1887 -	
54 & 55 Vict. c. 17.	-	The Charitable Trusts (Recovery) Act, 1891.	
57 & 58 Vict. c. 35.		The Charitable Trusts (Places of Religious Worship) Amendment Act, 1894.	
.	.	.	.

(b.) EXTENT OF ACTS.

[C. T. Act, 1853.] 67. This Act shall not extend to Scotland or Ireland. *Extent of Act.*

[C. T. Act, 1869.] 2. This Act shall not extend to Scotland or Ireland. *Extent of Act.*

[C. T. Act, 1891.] 7. This Act shall not extend to Scotland or Ireland. *Extent of Act.*

[C. T. Act, 1894.] 2. This Act shall not extend to Scotland or Ireland. *Extent of Act.*

(c.) INTERPRETATION OF TERMS.

[C. T. Act, 1853.] 66. In the Construction of this Act, except where the Context or other Provisions of the Act may require a different Construction, *the Expression " Court of Chancery" shall mean and include the Master of the Rolls and every Judge of the Court of Chancery in England ;* the Expression " Lord Chancellor" shall mean and include the Lord Chancellor of Great Britain and the Lord Keeper and the Commissioners of the Great Seal of Great Britain for the Time being; the Expressions " District Court of Bankruptcy" and " District Court" shall mean and include every District Court of Bankruptcy established or to be established under the Act of the Fifth and Sixth Years of the Reign of Her present Majesty, Chapter Twenty-two, or under any other Act or Acts passed or to be passed for the Alteration or Amendment or the Extension of the same Act, or for the Establishment of any District Court or Courts of Bankruptcy in England or Wales, and every Commissioner or Judge of every such District Court ;† the Expression " County Court" shall mean and include every County Court holden or established or to be holden or established under the Act of the Ninth and Tenth Years of Her Majesty,* *Interpretation of Terms.*

[* Repealed by the Statute Law Revision Act, 1892 (55 & 56 Vict. c. 19.).]
[† Repealed by the Statute Law Revision Act, 1875 (38 & 39 Vict. c. 66.).]

Chapter Ninety-five, or any Act or Acts passed or to be passed for the Alteration or Extension of the same Act, and every Judge of any such Court: The expression "Charity" shall mean every endowed Foundation and Institution taking or to take Effect in England or Wales, and coming within the Meaning, Purview, or Interpretation of the Statute of the Forty-third Year of Queen Elizabeth, Chapter Four, or as to which, or the Administration of the Revenues or Property whereof, the Court of Chancery has or may exercise Jurisdiction; the Expression "Trustee" of any Charity shall mean and include every Person and Corporation seised or possessed of or entitled to any Real or Personal Estate, or any Interest therein, in trust for or for the Benefit of such Charity, or all or any of the Objects or Purposes thereof, and every Member of any such Corporation; and the Expression "the Board" shall mean the said Charity Commissioners sitting as a Board under this Act; and the Expression "Endowment" shall mean and include all Lands and Real Estate whatsoever, of any Tenure, and any Charge thereon, or Interest therein, and all Stocks, Funds, Monies, Securities, Investments, and Personal Estate whatsoever, which shall for the Time being belong to or be held in trust for any Charity, or for all or any of the Objects or Purposes thereof; *and the Expression "Land" shall extend to and include Manors, Messuages, Buildings, Tenements, and Hereditaments, corporeal and incorporeal, of every Tenure and Description.*†

As to the Term "Charity." — [C. T. Act, 1855.] 48. In the Construction of the principal Act and this Act the Word "Charity" shall include every Institution in England or Wales endowed for charitable Purposes, but shall not include any Charity or Institution expressly exempted from the Operation of the Act of 1853, and Words applying to any Person or Individual shall apply also to a Corporation, whether sole or aggregate.

Interpretation. — [C. T. Act, 1891.] 2. In this Act, unless the context requires otherwise,—

The expression "the Board" means the Charity Commissioners for England and Wales:

The expression "prescribed" means prescribed by rules made under the provisions of this Act.

II.—Exemptions from the Jurisdiction created by the Charitable Trusts Acts, and Incidental Provisions.

Exemptions from the Operation of Act. — [C. T. Act, 1853.] 62. This Act shall not extend to the Universities of Oxford, Cambridge, London, or Durham, or any College or Hall in the said Universities of Oxford, Cambridge, and Durham, or to any Cathedral or Collegiate Church, or to any Building registered as a Place of Meeting for Religious Worship with the Registrar General of Births, Deaths, or Marriages in England and Wales, and bonâ fide used as a Place of Meeting for Religious Worship; *nor shall this Act, for the Period of Two Years from the passing thereof, extend or be in any Manner applied to Charities or Institutions, the Funds or Income of which are applicable exclusively for the Benefit of Persons of the Roman Catholic Persuasion, and which are under the Superintendence or Control of Persons of that Persuasion,*‡ nor shall this Act extend or be applied to the Commissioners of Queen Anne's Bounty, or to the British Museum, or to any Friendly or Benefit Society, or Savings Bank, or any Institution, Establishment, or Society for religious or other charitable Purposes, or to the Auxiliary or Branch Associations connected therewith, wholly maintained by voluntary Contributions, or any Bookselling or Publishing Business carried on by or under the Direction of any Society

---

[* *Repealed by the Statute Law Revision Act,* 1892 (55 & 56 *Vict. c.* 19.) ; *definition now supplied by the Interpretation Act,* 1889, *sect.* 6 (52 & 53 *Vict. c.* 63.).]
[† *Repealed by the Statute Law Revision Act,* 1892 (55 & 56 *Vict. c.* 19.) ; *definition now supplied by the Interpretation Act,* 1889, *sect.* 3 (52 & 53 *Vict. c.* 63.).]
[‡ *Repealed by the Statute Law Revision Act,* 1875 (38 & 39 *Vict. c.* 66.).]

wholly or partially exempted from this Act, so far as such Business is or shall be carried on by means of voluntary Contributions only, or the Capital or Stock of such Business; and where any Charity is maintained partly by voluntary Subscriptions and partly by Income arising from any Endowment, the Powers and Provisions of the Act, shall, with respect to such Charity, extend and apply to the Income from Endowment only, to the Exclusion of voluntary Subscriptions, and the Application thereof; and no Donation or Bequest unto or in trust for any such Charity as last aforesaid, of which no special Application or Appropriation shall be directed or declared by the Donor or Testator, and which may legally be applied by the governing or managing Body of such Charity as Income in aid of the voluntary Subscriptions, shall be subject to the Jurisdiction or Control of the said Board, or the Powers or Provisions of this Act; and no Portion of any such Donation or Bequest as last aforesaid, or of any voluntary Subscription, which is now or shall or may from Time to Time be set apart or appropriated and invested by the governing or managing Body of the Charity, for the Purpose of being held and applied or expended for or to some defined and specific Object or Purpose connected with such Charity, in pursuance of any Rule or Resolution made or adopted by the governing or managing Body of such Charity, or of any Donation or Bequest in aid of any Fund so set apart or appropriated for any such Object or Purpose as aforesaid, shall be subject to the Jurisdiction or Control of the said Board or the Powers or Provisions of this Act; and nothing in this Act shall subject the Funds or Property of any Missionary or other similar Society, or the Missionaries, Teachers or Officers of such Society, or of any Branch thereof, which Funds or Property shall not be within the Limits of England or Wales, to the Jurisdiction of the said Board: Provided always, that the said Exemption shall not extend to any Cathedral, Collegiate, Chapter or other Schools.

Provisions as to Charities supported partly by voluntary Subscriptions.

[C. T. Act, 1855.] 47. *Neither this Act nor the principal Act shall, until the First Day of September One thousand eight hundred and fifty-six, extend or be in any Manner applied to Charities or Institutions the Funds or Income of which are applicable exclusively for the Benefit of Persons of the Roman Catholic Persuasion, and which are under the Superintendence and Control of Persons of that Persuasion,* nor shall anything in this Act extend to any of the Cases which by the Sixty-second Section of the principal Act are excepted from the Operation thereof.*

Acts not to apply to Roman Catholic Charities until 1st Sept. 1856.

[C. T. Act, 1855.] 49. Nothing in this Act or in the principal Act contained shall extend to the Colleges of Eton and Winchester, or either of them.

Act not to extend to Eton or Winchester.

[C. T. Act, 1894.] 4. The exemption of any building registered as a place of meeting for religious worship with the Registrar-General of Births, Deaths, or Marriages in England and Wales, and bonâ fide used as a place of meeting for religious worship, contained in the sixty-second section of the Charitable Trusts Act, 1853, and in the ninth section of the Places of Worship Registration Act, 1855, shall extend, and shall, without prejudice to any order of the Charity Commissioners made before the passing of this Act, be deemed to have always extended to—

Extension of exemption in 16 & 17 Vict. c. 137 s. 62. 18 & 19 Vict c. 81. s. 9, of places of meeting for religious worship.

(a) any forecourt, yard, garden, burial-ground, vestry, or caretaker's house, in respect of situation connected with, and held upon the same trusts as, any building registered and bonâ fide used as aforesaid; and

(b) any Sunday-school house or other land or building which shall be certified by an order of the Charity Commissioners, made upon the application of one or more of the trustees or persons acting in the administration thereof, to be held upon the same trusts as any building registered and used as aforesaid, or upon like trusts, and to be in respect of situation so connected with or held or used in connexion with such building that it cannot conveniently be separated therefrom: . . .

[*This section is printed in full at p. 39.*]

[* *Repealed by the Statute Law Revision Act,* 1875 (38 & 39 *Vict. c.* 66.).]

Exempted Charities may petition Commissioners to have Benefit of Act.

[C. T. Act, 1853.] 63. *It shall be lawful for any of the Charities exempted from the Operation of this Act, by Order or Resolution duly made in conformity with the Constitution or Rules of such Charity (and which in that Case only shall be binding), to apply by Petition to the Commissioners to have the Benefit of this Act, either generally or as to any of the Provisions herein contained ; and such Petition shall be under the Seal of such Charity if incorporated, and if not then under the Hands of the major Part of the Trustees and governing Body of such Charity ; and in such Case it shall be lawful for the Commissioners, if they shall think fit, to make an Order in conformity with such Application, and such Charity shall thenceforth be entitled to and be bound by all the Provisions of this Act, if admitted generally thereto, or by such of the Enactments thereof, as shall be mentioned and specified in such Order of the Commissioners, but in either Case in the same Manner as if such Charity had not been exempted from this Act, or such Exemption had not extended to the Enactments specified in such Order.*

Application by exempted charities to have benefit of Act. See 16 & 17 Vict. c. 137. s. 63.

[C. T. Act, 1869.] 14. Either the trustees or the persons acting in the administration of any charity exempted from the operation of the Charitable Trusts Acts, 1853 to 1869, may apply to the Board to have the said Acts or any provisions thereof specified in the application extended to such charity: Such application shall be made by such of the said trustees or persons as having regard to the value of the charity might under the provisions of the said Acts, if the charity were not exempted therefrom, make an application for a scheme to any judge or court or to the Board, and shall be made in the same manner and according to the same regulations as such application.

On any such application the Board may make an order directing that the said Acts or any provisions of them specified in the application shall extend, and such Acts or provisions shall thereupon after the date of the order extend to such charity in the same manner as if it were not exempted therefrom.

Before making any order under this section the Board shall cause such notices of the proposed order to be given as by section three of the Charitable Trusts Act, 1860, as amended by this Act, and by section six of the same Act are required to be given before the making of an order for establishing a scheme.†

Extension of part of Acts to registered places of religious worship.

[C. T. Act, 1869.] 15. So much of the Charitable Trusts Acts, 1853 to 1869, as authorises and relates to orders of the Board for the appointment or removal of trustees of a charity, or for or relating to the vesting of any real or personal estate belonging thereto, or for the establishment of any scheme for the administration of any charity, shall extend to buildings registered as places of meeting for religious worship with the Registrar General of Births, Deaths, or Marriages in England, and bonâ fide used as places of meeting for religious worship: Provided that no such order shall be made except upon the application of the trustees or persons acting in the administration of the charity, made in manner provided by section four of the Charitable Trusts Act, 1860, or by this Act.‡ Save as provided by this section, such buildings shall continue exempted from the Charitable Trusts Acts, 1853 to 1869.

32 & 33 Vict. c. 110. s. 15.

[C. T. Act, 1894.] 4. . . . . Provided always that so much of the Charitable Trusts Acts, 1853 to 1891, as by virtue of the fifteenth section of the Charitable Trusts Act, 1869, extends to buildings registered and used as aforesaid, shall also extend to the properties declared to be exempted by

[* *Repealed by the Charitable Trusts Act,* 1869, *sect.* 17 (*p.* 72).]
[† *For the sections here referred to, viz., sections* 3 *and* 6 *of the Charitable Trusts Act,* 1860, *and section* 4 *of the Charitable Trusts Act,* 1869. *see p.* 55 *and* 75.]
[‡ *For the sections here referred to, viz., section* 4 *of the Charitable Trusts Act,* 1860, *and section* 5 *of the Charitable Trusts Act,* 1869, *see p.* 45.]

this Act in the same manner and subject to the same restrictions as the buildings registered and used as aforesaid.

[*This section is printed in full at p* 39.]

III.—Constitution, Salaries, and Procedure of the Charity Commissioners, and their Officers, &c.; Scale of Fees for Business; Annual Report.

(*a.*) CONSTITUTION.

[**C. T. Act, 1853.**] **1.** It shall be lawful for Her Majesty *and Her Successors,** by Warrant under the Royal Sign Manual, to appoint Four Commissioners,† and also One Secretary *and Two Inspectors‡* for the Purposes of this Act, and upon any Vacancy by the Death, Resignation, or Removal of any Commissioner, Secretary, *or Inspector‡* under this Act, from Time to Time in like Manner to appoint another Person to succeed to such Vacancy, and until a fresh Appointment shall be made it shall be lawful for the surviving or continuing Commissioners, in case of any Vacancy, to act as if no such Vacancy had occurred; and Three of the said Commissioners shall hold Office during good Behaviour; and the Fourth, and every Secretary *and Inspector‡* to be appointed under this Act, shall hold Office during the Pleasure of Her Majesty.

Her Majesty empowered to appoint Charity Commissioners, Secretary, and Inspectors.

[**C. T. Act, 1853.**] **2.** The said Three Commissioners so holding Office during good Behaviour shall be paid as herein-after mentioned, and Two at least of the said paid Commissioners for the time being shall be Barristers-at-Law of not less than Twelve Years standing at the Time of their respective Appointments, and One of such Barristers shall be the Chief Commissioner, and shall be so called and distinguished in his Appointment.

Qualification of Commissioners.

[**C. T. Act, 1855.**] **3.** *It shall be lawful for Her Majesty and Her Successors, under the Royal Sign Manual, to appoint additional Inspectors (not exceeding three in Number) for the Purposes of this Act and the Charitable Trusts Act, 1853, and such additional Inspectors shall hold office during Pleasure, and shall be possessed of the same Powers, Authorities, and Jurisdiction, and be entitled to the same Privileges and Emoluments, as the Inspectors appointed under the said former Act of One Thousand eight hundred and fifty-three.§*

Power to appoint additional Inspectors.

[**C. T. Act, 1887.**] **2.**—(1.) The Charity Commissioners for England and Wales (in this Act referred to as "the Board") may from time to time with the approval in each case of the Commissioners of Her Majesty's Treasury (in this Act referred to as the Treasury) appoint assistant commissioners, and may remove any such assistant commissioner.

Appointment of assistant commissioners.

(2.) The number [and salaries] of the assistant commissioners under this Act shall be such as the Treasury may from time to time sanction.

(3.) Each assistant commissioner under this Act shall have the same powers as an inspector under the Charitable Trusts Acts, 1853 to 1869, and the sections of the Charitable Trusts Acts, 1853 to 1869, specified in the First Schedule to this Act, shall have effect as if "assistant commissioner" or "assistant commissioners" were therein substituted for "inspector" or "inspectors," as the case may be, and each assistant commissioner acting under the authority of the Board may exercise the said powers for any purpose of or incidental to any duties imposed on the Board by Parliament under any present or future Act.

[* *Repealed by the Statute Law Revision Act,* 1892 (55 & 56 *Vict. c.* 19).]

[† *As to the appointment of two additional Charity Commissioners under the Endowed Schools Act,* 1871, *see section* 2 *of that Act, the provisions of which are printed in Appendix No.* 2 (*p.* 77).]

[‡ *Repealed by the Charitable Trusts Act,* 1887, *sect.* 6 (*p.* 72).]

[§ *Repealed by the Statute Law Revision Act,* 1875 (38 & 39 *Vict. c.* 66).]

(4.) The power of appointing inspectors under the Charitable Trusts Acts, 1853 to 1869, shall cease.

SCHEDULES.

FIRST SCHEDULE.

SECTIONS OF CHARITABLE TRUSTS ACTS RELATING TO INSPECTORS AND APPLIED TO ASSISTANT COMMISSIONERS.

Session and Chapter.	Title of Act.	Sections applied.
16 & 17 Vict. c. 137.	The Charitable Trusts Act, 1853	Sections five, nine, ten, eleven, twelve, fourteen, fifteen, nineteen, twenty-three, fifty-four, fifty-six, fifty-seven, and fifty-eight.
18 & 19 Vict. c. 124.	The Charitable Trusts Amendment Act, 1855.	Sections six, seven, and eight.
23 & 24 Vict. c. 136.	The Charitable Trusts Act, 1860	Section six.
32 & 33 Vict. c. 110.	The Charitable Trusts Act, 1869	Section nine.

No paid Commissioner, Secretary, or Inspector, to sit in House of Commons.

[C. T. Act, 1853.] **5.** No paid Commissioner, Secretary, or *Inspector** to be appointed under this Act shall be capable of sitting in the House of Commons during the Tenure of his Office.

Commissioners, &c. exempted from serving on Juries.

[C. T. Act, 1860.] **24.** *Every Commissioner, Secretary, and Inspector acting under or employed for the Purposes of the said Acts shall be exempt from serving on Juries while he shall be so acting or employed.†*

Officers of the Board.

[C. T. Act, 1853.] **3.** The said Commissioners, with the Sanction of the *Commissioners of Her Majesty's‡* Treasury, shall from Time to Time appoint such Clerks and Messengers as the said Commissioners may think fit, and all Persons appointed under this Provision shall hold their Offices during the Pleasure of the said Commissioners.

(b.) SALARIES.

Salaries.

[C. T. Act, 1853.] **4.** *There shall be paid to the said paid Commissioners, and to the said Secretary, Inspectors, Clerks, and Messengers, such Salaries not exceeding for the Chief Commissioner the annual sum of One thousand five hundred Pounds, and for each of the other paid Commissioners the annual sum of One thousand two hundred pounds, and for the said Secretary the annual Sum of Six hundred Pounds, and for each of the said Inspectors the annual Sum of Eight hundred Pounds, as shall be from Time to Time allowed by the Commissioners of Her Majesty's Treasury, who may also allow to every Commissioner, Inspector, and other Person appointed for the Purposes of this Act such reasonable Travelling and other Expenses as may be incurred by him in the Execution of his Office, and the said Salaries and Expenses, and the incidental Expenses of the said Board, shall be paid out of any Monies which may be from Time to Time provided by Parliament for that Purpose: Provided always, that after the Thirty-first day of March, in the Year One thousand eight hundred and fifty-seven, the said annual Salary shall be paid to One only of the said Commissioners besides the said Chief Commissioner.§*

[* Note "Assistant Commissioner." See Charitable Trusts Act, 1887, sect. 2, sub-section 3 (p. 13).]
[† Repealed by the Statute Law Revision Act, 1875 (38 & 39 Vict. c. 66.) as being inconsistent with sect. 9 of the Jurors Act, 1870 (33 & 34 Vict. c. 77.).]
[‡ Repealed by the Statute Law Revision Act, 1892 (55 & 56 Vict. c. 19.).]
[§ This section is wholly repealed by the Charitable Trusts Act, 1887, sect. 6 (p. 72).]

[C. T. Act, 1855.] 2. *So much of·the principal Act (Section IV.) as* *provides that after the Thirty-first Day of March One thousand eight hundred* *and fifty-seven an annual Salary shall be paid to One only of the Commis-* *sioners besides the Chief Commissioner is hereby repealed.**

Provision as to the Salary of One of the Commissioners repealed.

[C. T. Act, 1860.] 22. *There shall be paid to the Secretary for the* *Time being of the said Commissioners, in consideration of the Increase and* *Extent of his Official duties, such a Salary, not exceeding the annual Sum of* *Eight hundred Pounds, in lieu of the Salary payable to him under the firstly* *cited Act, as shall from Time to Time be allowed by the Commissioners of* *Her Majesty's Treasury.†*

Salary of the Secretary.

[Endowed Schools Act, 1874 (37 & 38 Vict. c. 87.).] 3. *There* *shall be repealed so much of the Charitable Trusts Acts,* 1853 *to* 1869, *as* *regulates the amounts of the salaries of the Commissioners, their secretary* *and inspectors; and‡* there shall be paid to the Commissioners, their secretary or secretaries, assistant commissioners, inspectors, officers, and clerks, whether appointed under this Act or under the said Charitable Trusts Acts, out of moneys provided by Parliament, such salaries as the Treasury may from time to time determine : Provided that no decrease shall be made in pursuance of this section in the salary of any Charity Commissioner, secretary, inspector, officer, or clerk appointed before the passing of this Act under the said Charitable Trusts Acts, or any of them.

Salaries of Charity Commissioners and their officers.

[C. T. Act, 1887.] 2.—(2.) The . . . . salaries of the assistant commissioners under this Act shall be such as the Treasury may from time to time sanction.

Appointment of assistant commissioners.

[*This section is printed in full at p. 13.*]

(c.) PROCEDURE, &c.

[C. T. Act, 1853.] 6. The said Commissioners to be appointed under this Act shall be styled "The Charity Commissioners for England and Wales," and may have and use a Seal for authenticating Documents, and such Commissioners shall sit from Time to Time as a Board for carrying this Act into execution ; and any Two of such Commissioners may form a Board, and may exercise all or any of the Powers conferred on the Commissioners or the Board by this Act.

Style of Commissioners, who may sit as a Board.

[C. T. Act, 1853.] 7. The said Board shall, by General Minutes, from Time to Time prescribe Regulations for their Proceedings, and the Proceedings of their Inspectors, and concerning the Form and Manner of Applications to the said Board, and the Conditions to be performed by Applicants, and for the Guidance of Applicants in relation thereto, and all such General Minutes shall be signed by Three of the said Commissioners at the least ; and Copies of all such General Minutes shall be laid before both Houses of Parliament within Fourteen Days after the making thereof, if Parliament be sitting, or if Parliament be not sitting, then within Fourteen Days after the next meeting thereof.

Board to frame General Minutes.

[C. T. Act, 1860.] 21. The said Board shall from Time to Time make such Minutes as shall be required relative to the Institution and Conduct of their Proceedings under the Jurisdiction created by this Act.

Board to make Minutes.

[C. T. Act, 1853.] 8. The said Board shall cause Minutes of their Proceedings, and all Orders, Certificates, and Schemes, made or approved by them under this Act, to be entered in Books to be provided and kept for such Purpose, and all such Entries shall be signed by their Secretary, and all Copies purporting to be extracted from the Books of the said Board, and to be certified by their Secretary, of any such Minutes, Orders, Certificates,

Minutes of Proceedings and Orders, &c. to be entered, and Copies of Entries

---

[* *Repealed by the Statute Law Revision Act,* 1875 (38 & 39 Vict. c. 66.).]
[† *Repealed by the Endowed Schools Act,* 1874, sect. 3 (37 & 38 Vict. c. 87.).]
[‡ *Repealed by the Statute Law Revision Act,* 1883 (46 & 47 Vict. c 39.).]

signed by the Secretary to be received in Evidence.

and Schemes entered as aforesaid, shall be received as Evidence of the Proceedings to which such Minutes shall relate, and of such Orders, Certificates, or Schemes, and of the making or Approval thereof (as the case may require) by the said Board, without further Proof thereof.

The Acts of the Board, how to be authenticated.

[C. T. Act, 1855.]   4. Every Act of the Board may be sufficiently authenticated by the Seal of the Commissioners, and the Signature of their Secretary, *or in his Absence of the Chief Clerk.**

Entries in and Extracts from the Books of the Board, how to be authenticated.

[C. T. Act, 1855.]   5. All Orders, Certificates, Schemes, and other Documents issued under the Seal of the Board shall be deemed and taken to be the Originals, and Copies thereof shall be entered in the Books of the Board, and all such Entries may be sufficiently certified by the Signature of the Secretary, *or in his Absence of the Chief Clerk :** Every Order, Certificate, Scheme, and other Document purporting to be sealed with the Seal of the Board shall be received in Evidence without further Proof; and any Writing purporting to be a Copy extracted from the said Books, and to be certified as aforesaid, shall be received in Evidence in like Manner.

Provision for absence of secretary.

[C. T. Act, 1887.]   3. The signature of any officer of the Board (whether assistant secretary or other) who for the time being is authorised by an order of the Board signed by two Commissioners to act on behalf of the secretary of the Board shall, for all purposes of the Charitable Trusts Acts, 1853 to 1869, or any other enactment, be as valid as the signature of the secretary; and a reference in any enactment to the signature of the secretary shall include a reference to the signature of such officer, and any document signed by an officer expressed to be so authorised shall be received in evidence without proof of the authority.

Mode of application to Board.

[C. T. Act, 1869.]   5. An application to the Board of Charity Commissioners for England and Wales, for the purposes of the Charitable Trusts Acts, 1853 to 1869, when made by the trustees or persons acting in the administration of the charity, may be made in writing signed by any person authorised in that behalf by a resolution passed by a majority of those trustees or persons who are present at a meeting of their body duly constituted and vote on the question.

Powers of Board on application.

[C. T. Act, 1869.]   6. The Board shall be deemed to have and to have always had power in any order made upon an application to them, for the exercise of their jurisdiction under the Charitable Trusts Acts, 1853 to 1869, to insert in the order any incidental provisions which they think expedient for carrying into effect the substantial objects of the application, and which they would have had power to insert if such provisions had been included in the application.

Discharge of order of Board for irregularity.

[C. T. Act, 1869.]   8. The Board shall be deemed to have and to have always had power with or without any application to discharge, within twelve months after an order is made by them, the whole or any part of any order appearing to have been made by them by mistake or on misrepresentation, or otherwise than in conformity with the Charitable Trusts Acts, 1853 to 1869.

Every order made by the Board, in exercising their jurisdiction under the Charitable Trusts Acts, 1853 to 1869, shall, until discharged or varied by the Board or by the Court of Chancery on appeal under section eight of the Charitable Trusts Act, 1860,† have effect according to its tenor.

Every order of the Board shall, subject to all powers which the Court of Chancery has to discharge or vary it, under section eight of the Charitable Trusts Act, 1860,† and subject to the power of the Board to discharge it wholly or partially for the causes mentioned in this section, be deemed to have been duly and formally made, and no objection thereto on the ground only of irregularity or informality shall be entertained.

[* *Repealed by the Charitable Trusts Act, 1887, sect. 6 (p. 72).*]
[† *This section is printed in full in Appendix, No. 1, p. 75.*]

[C. T. Act, 1855.]   9. Any Person refusing or wilfully neglecting to comply . . . . with any Order of the Board, made under the Provisions of this Act or the principal Act,* . . . . shall be taken to be guilty of a Contempt of the High Court of Chancery, and shall be liable to be attached and committed by such Court, on summary Application by the Commissioners to the same Court or to any Judge thereof, and shall pay such Costs attending such Contempt as the said Court or Judge shall direct: Provided always, that the Court may at any Time discharge, on such Terms as it may deem just, any Person attached or committed on any such application, ... *Persons not complying with requisitions. &c. to be deemed guilty of a Contempt of the Court of Chancery.*

[This section is printed in full at p. 20.]

[C. T. Act, 1860.]   20. All Orders made by the said Board under the Provisions of this Act shall be enforceable by the same Means, and shall be subject to the same Provisions, as are applicable under the Charitable Trusts Act, 1853, and the Charitable Trusts Amendment Act, 1855, respectively, to any Orders of the said Board made thereunder. *Orders to be enforceable as under former Acts.*

(d.) SCALE OF FEES FOR BUSINESS.

[C. T. Act, 1869.]   16. *The Commissioners of Her Majesty's†* Treasury may from time to time prescribe a scale of fees to be charged for any business done by the Board under this or any other Act, *and may direct whether the same shall be imposed by stamps or otherwise, and by whom and in what manner the same shall be collected, accounted for, and appropriated ;‡* and before any such fees shall be taken or received by the said Charity Commissioners every such scale of fees shall be published in the London Gazette. The scale of fees shall be laid before both Houses of Parliament within thirty days after the same has been so prescribed if Parliament is then sitting, and if not, within thirty days after the then next meeting of Parliament ; and if any such scale shall be disapproved of by both Houses of Parliament, within one month after the same shall have been so laid before Parliament, such fees or such parts thereof as shall be disapproved of shall not be charged by the Board. *Treasury to fix scale of fees. Scale to be laid before Parliament.*

(e.) ANNUAL REPORT.

[C. T. Act, 1853.]   60. The said Board shall in the Month of February in every Year make a Report to Her Majesty of all their Proceedings during the Preceding Year up to the Thirty-first Day of December then last past, and such Report shall, within Fourteen Days after the making thereof, be laid before both Houses of Parliament, if Parliament be then sitting, or otherwise within Fourteen Days after the Meeting thereof; and in such Report the said Board shall specially distinguish and set forth in full all the Schemes (if any) approved by them under the Provisions lastly herein-before contained,§ together with the Grounds of such their Approval, and the Objections (if any) which have been made thereto, and all Proceedings had in respect of such Objections and the Grounds on which any such Objections have been over-ruled; . . . . . *Annual Report to be laid before Parliament which shall set forth all the Schemes approved.*

[This section is printed in full at p. 53.]

[* *i.e., the Charitable Trusts Act,* 1853.]
[† *Repealed by the Statute Law Revision (No. 2) Act,* 1893 (56 & 57 *Vict. c.* 54.).]
[‡ *Repealed by the Statute Law Revision Act,* 1883 (46 & 47 *Vict. c.* 39.).]
[§ *The Schemes here referred to are Schemes provisionally approved by the Charity Commissioners to be laid before Parliament : see sections* 54–59 *of the Charitable Trusts Act,* 1853 (*p.* 52).]

IV.—Provisions conferring on the Charity Commissioners, and their Officers, Powers of Inquiry, and of compelling production of Accounts and Documents, and imposing on Trustees of Charities the Duty of keeping and rendering Accounts.

(a.) *POWERS OF INQUIRY, &c. OF THE CHARITY COMMISSIONERS AND THEIR OFFICERS.*

Board to inquire into Condition and Management of Charities.

[**C. T. Act, 1853.**] **9.** It shall be lawful for the said Board from Time to Time, as they in their Discretion may see fit, to examine and inquire into all or any Charities in England or Wales, and the Nature and Objects, Administration, Management, and Results thereof, and the Value, Condition, Management, and Application of the Estates, Funds, Property, and Income belonging thereto; and the said Board may cause Examinations and Inquiries in relation to the Matters aforesaid to be made and prosecuted by their *Inspectors*,* acting together or separately, in such Cases and at such Times as the said Board may think fit; and all such *Inspectors** shall from Time to Time report their Proceedings to the said Board.

Power to require Accounts and Statements.

[**C. T. Act, 1853.**] **10.** The said Board may require all Trustees or Persons acting or having any Concern in the Management or Administration of any Charity, or the Estates, Funds, or Property thereof, to render to the said Board, or to their *Inspectors*,* or either of them, Accounts and Statements in Writing in relation to such Charity, or the Funds, Estates, Property, Income, or Monies thereof, or the Administration, Management, and Application thereof, and may also require such Trustees and Persons to return Answers in Writing to any Questions or Inquiries addressed to them by the Direction of the said Board relating to the Matters aforesaid.

Officers having Custody of Records to furnish Copies and Extracts, if required by Board.

[**C. T. Act, 1853.**] **11.** All Officers having the Custody of Enrolments, Decrees, Reports, Records, and other Documents relating to or concerning any Charity shall furnish such Copies or Extracts as shall be required by the said Board; and every *Inspector*,* Secretary, and other Officer of the said Board for the Time being employed for the Purposes of this Act shall be at liberty, by the Authority and under the Directions of the Board, and subject to such Regulations as the Board may make in that Behalf, to examine and search the Registers and Records of every Court of Law and Equity, and every Ecclesiastical Court, and every public Registry and Office of Records, and to take Copies of and Extracts from any Decree or Document recorded or registered or deposited therein respectively, for any Purpose contemplated by this Act, without Fee or other Payment in respect thereof.

Inspector may examine Witnesses on Oath.

[**C. T. Act, 1853.**] **12.** Any *Inspector** acting under the Authority of the said Board may, by Precept under his Hand, subject to such Regulations as the said Board may make in that Behalf, require any Person, being a Trustee of any Charity or otherwise acting or having any Concern in the Management or Administration of any Charity, or of the Estates, Funds, or Property thereof, or in the Receipt or Payment of the Income or Monies thereof, or deriving any Income or Stipend therefrom, to attend before such *Inspector** for the Purpose of being examined by him touching or relating to such Charity, or the Estates, Funds, Property, or Income thereof, at any Time and Place mentioned or appointed by such Precept, and to bring and produce any Deed, Paper, Writing, Instrument, or other Document, being in the Custody, Possession, or Power of such Person, and relating to such Charity, or the Estates, Funds, Property, or Income thereof and may examine upon Oath all Persons attending in pursuance of such Precept,

[* Now "*Assistant Commissioners*" or "*Assistant Commissioner*," as context may require. See *Charitable Trusts Act*, 1887, sect. 2, subs. 3 (*p.* 13).]

and all Persons voluntarily attending before him, and may administer such Oath : Provided always, that no Person shall be obliged to travel in obedience to any such Precept more than Ten Miles from his Place of Abode.

[C. T. Act, 1853.] 13. If any Person wilfully give false Evidence upon any Examination under this Act, every Person so offending shall be deemed guilty of a Misdemeanor.

Persons giving false Evidence guilty of a Misdemeanor.

[C. T. Act, 1853.] 14. If any Person from whom the said Board, or any *Inspector*,* is authorized to require any Account or Statement or Answers to any Questions or Inquiries, or whose Attendance any *Inspector** is authorized to require, shall refuse or wilfully neglect to render to the said Board such Account or Statement, or to make Answers to such Questions or Inquiries, or to attend in obedience to any lawful Precept of any *Inspector** or to give Evidence before him, or shall wilfully alter, destroy, withhold, or refuse to produce any Deed, Paper, Writing, Instrument, or other Document which may be lawfully required to be produced before any *Inspector** or the said Board, every Person so offending shall be deemed and taken to have been guilty of a Contempt of the High Court of Chancery, and shall be liable to be attached and committed by such Court on summary Application by the Commissioners to the same, and shall pay the Costs of and attending such Contempt as the said Court shall direct.

Person refusing to render Accounts,&c. to be deemed guilty of a Contempt of Court.

[C. T. Act, 1853.] 15. Provided always, That nothing herein contained shall extend to give to the said Board or their *Inspectors** any Power of requiring from any Person holding or claiming to hold any Property whatsoever adversely to any Charity, or free or discharged from any Charitable Trust or Charge, any Information, or the Production of any Deed or Document whatever in relation to the Property so held or claimed adversely, or any Charitable Trust or Charge alleged to affect the same.

Saving for Persons claiming adversely to Charities.

[C. T. Act, 1855.] 6. The Board, or any Commissioner or *Inspector*,* such *Inspector** acting under the Authority of the Board, may require written Accounts and Statements and Answers to Inquiries relating to any Charity, or the Property or Income thereof, to be rendered or made to them respectively by all or any of the following Persons; that is to say,

The Powers of the Commissioners and Inspectors to inquire into Charities extended.

Trustees or Persons acting or concerned in the Administration of the Charity, its Property or Income, or in the Receipt or Payment of any Monies thereof :

Agents of any such Trustees or Persons :

Depositaries of any Funds or Monies of the Charity :

Persons in the beneficial Receipt of any Funds thereof, or of any Income or Stipend therefrom :

Persons having the Possession or Control of any Documents concerning the Charity or any Property thereof ;

And the Board or the Commissioner or *Inspector** may require the Persons rendering or making any such Account, Statement, or Answer to verify the same by Oath or otherwise, and may administer such Oath : Provided always, that nothing herein contained shall extend to give to the said Board or their *Inspectors** any Power of requiring from any Person holding or claiming to hold any Property whatsoever adversely to any Charity, or free or discharged from any Charitable Trust or Charge, any Information, or the Production of any Deed or Document whatever, in relation to the Property so held or claimed adversely, or any Charitable Trust or Charge alleged to affect the same.

[C. T. Act, 1855.] 7. The Board, or any Commissioner or *Inspector** acting as aforesaid, may require all or any such Trustees and Persons as aforesaid to attend before them respectively at such Times and Places as may be reasonably appointed, for the Purpose of being examined in relation to the Charity, and to answer such Questions as may be proposed to

Power to require Trustees and others to attend and be examined

[* Now " *Assistant Commissioners* " or "*Assistant Commissioner,*" as context may require. See *Charitable Trusts Act,* 1887, *sect.* 2. *subs.* 3 (*p.* 13).]

them, and to produce upon such Examination any Documents in their Custody or Power relating to the Charity or the Property thereof, and may examine upon Oath or otherwise all such Persons and all Persons voluntarily attending, and may administer such Oath: Provided always, that no Person shall be obliged to travel in obedience to any such Requisition more than Ten Miles from his Place of Abode.

Precepts or Orders for the preceding Purposes, how to be made.

[**C. T. Act, 1855.**] 8. All Requisitions made under the foregoing Authorities shall be made respectively by the Order of the Board, or by Precept, under the Hand of the Commissioner or *Inspector** making the same.

Persons not complying with Requisitions, &c. to be deemed guilty of a Contempt of the Court of Chancery.

[**C. T. Act, 1855.**] 9. Any Person refusing or wilfully neglecting to comply with any such Requisition, or with any Order of the Board, made under the Provisions of this Act or the principal Act,† or destroying or withholding any Document required to be produced or transmitted by him, shall be taken to be guilty of a Contempt of the High Court of Chancery, and shall be liable to be attached and committed by such Court, on summary Application by the Commissioners to the same Court or to any Judge thereof, and shall pay such Costs attending such Contempt as the said Court or Judge shall direct: Provided always, that the Court may at any Time discharge, on such Terms as it may deem just, any Person attached or committed on any such Application, or on any Application made under Section Fourteen of the principal Act.‡

Employment of persons to prepare and defend scheme.

[**C. T. Act, 1869.**] 9. The Board, if they think it desirable, where the gross annual income of a Charity is in their opinion sufficient to bear the expense, may, upon the application of the Trustees or of any other person or persons entitled to apply to them in that behalf, ... order the costs incurred . . . . upon any inquiry by an inspector,* . . . . to be provided in the same manner as if they were costs of a transaction mentioned in section thirty-six of the Charitable Trusts Act, 1855.§

[*This section is printed in full at p. 26.*]

Power to require the Transmission of Documents belonging to Charities.

[**C. T. Act, 1860.**] 19. The Board may require any Person having the Custody or Control of any Deed or Document in which any Charity or Charities shall be solely interested to transmit the same to the Office of the said Commissioners for Examination; and where such Deed or Document shall not be held by any Person entitled as a Trustee or otherwise to the Custody thereof, the Board may either retain the same, for the Security thereof, in the Repository provided by them under the Sixty-third‖ Section of "The Charitable Trusts Act, 1853," or, as they may think most advantageous to the Charity, may thereupon, or at any Time thereafter, return or issue the same to the Trustees or Persons acting in the Administration of the Charity, for the Purposes thereof.

Orders to be enforceable as under former Acts.

[**C. T. Act, 1860.**] 20. All Orders made by the said Board under the Provisions of this Act shall be enforceable by the same Means, and shall be subject to the same Provisions, as are applicable under the Charitable Trusts Act, 1853, and the Charitable Trusts Amendment Act, 1855, respectively, to any Orders of the said Board made thereunder.¶

(b.) *DUTY OF TRUSTEES OF CHARITIES IN REGARD TO ACCOUNTS, &c.*

Accounts of Trustees of Charities to

[**C. T. Act, 1853.**] 61. The Trustees or Persons acting in the Administration of every Charity shall, in Books to be kept by them for that

---

[* *Now "Assistant Commissioners" or "Assistant Commissioner," as context may require. See Charitable Trusts Act, 1887, sect. 2, subs. 3 (p. 13).*]
[† *i.e., the Charitable Trusts Act, 1853.*]   [‡ *See preceding page.*]
[§ *For this section, see p. 26.*]   [‖ *Should be "Fifty-third" (see p. 42).*]
[¶ *See the Charitable Trusts Act, 1853, sect 14 (p. 19), and the Charitable Trusts Amendment Act, 1855, sect. 9 (supra).*]

Purpose, regularly enter or cause to be entered full and true Accounts of *be delivered to the Clerks of County Courts,* all Money received and paid respectively on account of such Charity,* *and on or before the Twenty-fifth Day of March in every Year, or on or before such other Day as shall or may be fixed and appointed for that Purpose by the said Board, shall cause a Statement in Writing to be made of the Income and Revenues, whether actually paid or then due, and the actual Receipts and Expenditure of such Charity for the Year ending on the Thirty-first Day of December then next preceding, or on some other convenient Day to be fixed and appointed for that Purpose by the said Board, and also a Balance Sheet containing a clear Statement of the Balance of such Account, which Statement and Balance Sheet respectively shall be certified under the Hand of some One or more of such Trustees or Persons (and audited by the Auditor of such Charity, if any there be) ; and as to every Charity whose gross annual Income for the Time being shall not exceed Thirty Pounds, every such Statement and Balance Sheet respectively, or a Duplicate or true Copy thereof respectively, shall be delivered or sent by such Trustees or Persons free of Charge to the Clerk of the County Court or some One of the County Courts (if more than One) to whose Jurisdiction such Charity may be subject under this Act (in case such Charity be subject to the Jurisdiction of any County Court under this Act), or if such Charity be not subject to the Jurisdiction of any County Court then to the Clerk of the County Court for the District or any One of the Districts (if more than One) wherein or nearest adjoining whereto such Charity is established, or the Property thereof (in whole or in part) is situate or administered and distributed ; and as to every Charity whose gross annual Income for the Time being shall exceed Thirty Pounds, every such Statement and Balance Sheet, or a Duplicate or true Copy thereof respectively (unless the said Board shall otherwise direct), shall be delivered or sent free of Charge to the Clerk of the Peace for the County or the Division of the County, or some One of the Counties or Divisions of Counties (if more than One) in which the Charity is established, or the Property thereof is wholly or partially situated or administered and distributed ; and every such Statement and Balance Sheet, or a Duplicate or true Copy thereof respectively, shall be kept and registered without Fee or Reward by the Registrar of County Courts Judgments or the Clerk of such County Court, and the Clerk of the Peace of such County or Division respectively, and shall be open to the Inspection of all Persons, at all seasonable Hours, on Payment of the Sum of One Shilling to the Registrar or Clerk for every such Inspection ; and any Person may require and have a Copy of any such Statement and Balance Sheet, or of any part thereof, paying therefor to such Registrar or Clerk after the Rate of Twopence for every Seventy-two Words or Figures; and a Duplicate or Copy of every such Statement and Balance Sheet to be made according to the foregoing Provision, so certified and audited as aforesaid, shall be delivered or transmitted, through the Post or otherwise, free of Charge, by such Trustees or other Persons, to the said Board, on or before the Twenty-fifth Day of March in every Year, or such other Day as may be fixed and appointed by the said Board as aforesaid ; and the said Board may from Time to Time by any Order direct that the Statement and Balance Sheet, or a Duplicate or true Copy thereof respectively, of the Accounts of any Charity whose gross annual Income exceeds Thirty Pounds shall be delivered or sent to the Clerk of the County Court in the same Manner as if the Income of such Charity did not exceed Thirty Pounds; and the said Board may make and give such further and other Orders and Directions in relation to the Delivery and Publication of such Accounts, and the Form thereof, as they may think fit, which Directions and Orders shall be obligatory on and obeyed by all such Trustees and Persons as aforesaid.

[**C. T. Act, 1855.**] 44. *Section Sixty-one of " The Charitable Trusts Act, 1853," except so much thereof as enacts that the Trustees or Persons acting in the administration of every Charity shall, in Books to be kept by them for that Purpose, regularly enter or cause to be entered full and true Accounts of all Money received and paid respectively on account of such* *Amendment of Sect. 61 of 16 & 17 Vict. c. 137, and other Provision made as to the*

[The rest of this section is repeated by the Charitable Trusts Amendment Act, 1855, sect. 44, infra.]*

C 3

Annual Returns of Accounts by Trustees of Charities.

Charity, shall be repealed as to all Accounts which such Trustees or Administrators shall not have been bound to render before the passing of this Act; and* the Trustees or Administrators of every Charity shall, on or before the Twenty-fifth Day of March One thousand eight hundred and fifty-six, prepare and make out and transmit to the Board an Account of the Endowments then belonging to the Charity, showing in the Case of Realty not in hand the Manner in which the same is let or occupied, and in the Case of Personalty the existing Investment or Employment thereof, and in what Names such Investments are made; and such Trustees or Administrators shall also on or before the Twenty-fifth Day of March next after the Acquisition of any Endowment not included in the foregoing Account prepare and make out, in like Manner, and transmit to the Board, a similar Account of such last-mentioned Endowment, and in case of any Alienation, or Charge, or Transfer of any Real or Personal Estate of the Charity, shall on or before the Twenty-fifth Day of March then next following transmit to the Board an Account of such Alienation, Charge, or Transfer, and such Trustees or Administrators shall also, on or before the Twenty-fifth day of March in every Year, or such other Day as may be fixed for that Purpose by the Board, or as may have been already fixed for rendering the Accounts thereof required by the principal Act, prepare, and make out the following Accounts in relation thereto; (that is to say,)

(1.) An Account of the gross Income arising from the Endowment, or which ought to have arisen therefrom during the Year ending on the Thirty-first Day of December then last, or on such other Day as may have been appointed for this Purpose by the Board:

(2.) An Account of all Balances in hand at the Commencement of the Year, and of all Monies received during the same Year on account of the Charity:

(3.) An Account for the same Period of all Payments:

(4.) An Account of all Monies owing to or from the Charity, so far as conveniently may be:

Which Accounts shall be certified under the Hand of One or more of the said Trustees or Administrators, and shall be audited by the Auditor of the Charity, if any; and the said Trustees or Administrators shall, within Fourteen Days after the Day appointed for making out such Accounts, deliver or transmit a Copy thereof to the Commissioners at their Office in London, and in the Case of Parochial Charities shall deliver another Copy thereof to the Churchwarden or Churchwardens of the Parish or Parishes with which the Objects of such Charities are identified, who shall present the same at the next General Meeting of the Vestry of such Parishes, and insert a Copy thereof in the Minutes of the Vestry Book; and every such Copy shall be open to the Inspection of all persons at all seasonable Hours, subject to such Regulations as to the said Board may seem fit; and any Person may require a Copy of every such Account, or of any Part thereof, on paying therefor after the Rate of Twopence for every Seventy-two Words or Figures.

[**Local Government Act, 1894 (56 & 57 Vict. c. 73.).**] **14.**—(6.) The accounts of all parochial charities, not being ecclesiastical charities, shall annually be laid before the parish meeting of any parish affected thereby, and the Charitable Trusts Amendment Act, 1855, shall apply, with the substitution in section forty-four of the parish meeting for the vestry, and of the chairman of the parish meeting for the churchwardens, and the names of the beneficiaries of dole charities shall be published annually in such form as the parish council, or where there is no parish council, the parish meeting, think fit.

Board may make Orders as to Delivery and Publication of Accounts by Trustees, &c.

[**C. T. Act, 1855.**] **45.** The Board may from Time to Time make such Orders as they may think fit in relation to the Delivery or Transmission of the said Accounts, and the Forms of such Accounts, and such Orders shall be executed by all Trustees and Persons from whom the Accounts to which they may relate are required.

[* *Repealed by the Statute Law Revision Act, 1875 (38 & 39 Vict. c. 66.).*]

V.—Provisions conferring on the Charity Commissioners Powers of Advice, and Arbitration, and of authorizing the Compromise of Claims by or against Charities, the Acquisition of Land, the Application of Funds, and certain other Acts of Trustees.

(a.) POWERS OF ADVICE.

[C. T. Act, 1853.] 16. The said Board shall receive and consider all Applications which may be made to them by any Trustee or other Person having any Concern in the Management or Administration of any Charity, for their Opinion, Advice, or Direction respecting such Charity, or the Management or Administration thereof, or the Estates, Funds, Property, or Income thereof, or the Application thereof, or any Question or Dispute relating to the same respectively, and, if they so think fit, may, upon any such Application, give such Opinion or Advice as they think expedient, subject to any Judicial Order or Direction which may be subsequently made or given by any competent Court or Judge; and such Opinion or Advice shall be in Writing, signed by Two or more of the said Commissioners, and sealed with the Seal of the said Commission;* and every Trustee and other Person who shall act upon or in accordance with the Opinion or Advice given by the said Board in respect of so acting be deemed and taken, so far as respects his own Responsibility, to have acted in accordance with his Trust; and no such Judicial Order or Direction subsequently made or given by any Court or Judge shall have any such retrospective Effect as to interfere with or impair the Indemnity by this Act given to Trustees and other Persons who have acted upon or in accordance with such Opinion or Advice of the said Board : Provided always, that nothing herein contained shall extend to indemnify any Trustee or other Person for any Act done in accordance with the Opinion or Advice of the said Board, if such Trustee or other Person have been guilty of any Fraud or wilful Concealment or Misrepresentation in obtaining such Opinion or Advice.

Board to entertain Applications for their Opinion or Advice.

Persons acting on Advice of Board to be indemnified.

[C. T. Act, 1853.] 19. Provided also, that . . . . the said Board, before giving any such Opinion, Advice, or Direction upon any such Application as aforesaid, ... , may, where local Inquiry appears to them to be requisite, cause such Inquiry to be made by One of their *Inspectors* ;† and the said Board may, in any Case where they see fit, before acting upon the Report of any *Inspector*,† cause such Report to be deposited for local Inspection, and give Notice of the same being so deposited, and consider any Statements or Objections which may be transmitted to them in relation thereto.

Board may, upon the Report of an Inspector, authorize Proceedings where no Notice has been given to them, and may in other Cases cause local Inquiries by their Inspector.

[*This section is printed in full at p. 60.*]

(b.) ARBITRAL POWERS.

[C. T. Act, 1853.] 64. Provided also, That if any Question or Dispute shall arise among the Members of any Charity *exempted from the Operation of this Act*‡ in relation to any Office, or the Fitness or Disqualification of any Trustee or Officer, or his Election or Removal, or generally in relation to the Management of the Charity, it shall be lawful for Two Thirds of the Members present at any Special Meeting, duly convened by Notice for the Purpose in the same Manner in which Meetings of such Charity are by the Rules thereof appointed to be held and convened, to refer such Question or Dispute to the Arbitration of the Commissioners, who

Disputes among Members of exempted Charities may be referred to Arbitration of Commissioners.

[* But see now Charitable Trusts Amendment Act, 1855, sect. 1 (p. 16), and Charitable Trusts Act, 1887, sect. 3 (p. 16).]
[† Now "Assistant Commissioner" or "Assistant Commissioners," as context may require. See Charitable Trusts Act, 1887, sect. 2, subs. 3 (p. 13).]
[‡ Repealed by the Statute Law Revision Act, 1875 (38 & 39 Vict. c. 66).]

C 4

shall accept such Reference and act therein as Arbitrators, and their Award shall be final, and may be made a Rule of Her Majesty's High Court of Chancery.

Application of Sect. 64, of 16 & 17 Vict. c. 137. [**C. T. Act, 1855.**] **46.** The Sixty-fourth Section of the principal Act shall apply as well to Members of any Charity within the Operation of that Act as to Members of any Charity exempted from the Operation thereof.

Power to ascertain Lands charged with Rents to Charities. [**C. T. Act, 1855.**] **33.** Where there shall be Uncertainty as to the specific Part of any Lands out of which any Rent, Annuity, or other periodical Payment, not exceeding the yearly Sum of Ten Pounds, charged upon some part of the same Lands, for the Benefit of a Charity, shall be payable, it shall be lawful for the Board, upon the Application of the Trustees or Persons acting in the Administration of the Charity, and with the Consent of the Persons interested, according to the aforesaid Definition of "Persons interested,"* in the same Lands, to determine by their Order the Land charged with such Rent, Annuity, or other periodical Payment, which shall thenceforth stand charged with such Rent, Annuity, or periodical Payment accordingly, to the Exoneration of the Residue of such Lands therefrom.

Expenses of Exchanges and Partitions, and determining Application of Charges. [**C. T. Act, 1855.**] **34.** The Expenses incident to the Application for and procuring of any such . . . . Order determining the Land charged with any Rent, Annuity, or periodical Payment, shall be paid by the Trustees or Administrators of the Charity, or by the other Parties to such Transactions, or by both, as the Board may direct.

[*This section is printed in full in Appendix, No. 1, p. 74.*]

(c.) *POWERS OF AUTHORIZING THE COMPROMISE OF CLAIMS BY OR AGAINST CHARITIES, THE ACQUISITION OF LAND, THE APPLICATION OF FUNDS, AND CERTAIN OTHER ACTS OF TRUSTEES.*

Board may sanction Compromise of Claims on behalf of Charity. [**C. T. Act, 1853.**] **23.** If in any Case it appear to the Trustees or Persons acting in the Administration of any Charity that any Claim or Demand or Cause of Suit against any Person in relation to such Charity may, with Advantage to the Charity, or should, under the special Circumstances of the Case, be compromised or adjusted without taking or without continuing any proceedings at Law or in Equity, such Trustees or Persons may, or the Person against whom such Claim, Demand, or Cause of Suit exists or is alleged to exist, may, with the Consent of the Trustees or Persons acting in the Administration of such Charity, submit to the said Board a Statement and Proposal for such Compromise or Adjustment; and if it appear to the said Board after such Inquiry in relation thereto by one of their *Inspectors,†* as they may deem requisite, or otherwise, that such Proposal, either with or without any Modification, is fit and proper, and for the Benefit of the Charity, it shall be lawful for the said Board to make such Order for and in relation to such Compromise or Adjustment as they may think fit; and upon the due Performance of the Terms and Conditions of such Compromise or Adjustment as aforesaid, such Agreement‡ shall be a final Bar to all Actions, Suits, Claims, and Demands by or on behalf of the Charity concerned therein, in respect to the Cause of Action, Suit, or Matter in respect to which such Compromise or Adjustment shall have been made.

[* *The Act contains no such "aforesaid definition." The definition referred to was contained in clause 41 of the Bill, as brought from the House of Lords, which was struck out in Committee of the House of Commons.*]
[† *Now "Assistant Commissioners." See Charitable Trusts Act, 1887, sect. 2, subs. 3 (p. 13).*]
[‡ *There is no previous mention of an "Agreement." The concluding paragraph of this section from "and upon the due performance," was not in the Bill as presented by the Lord Chancellor, but was introduced by a Select Committee of the House of Lords. The section, with this exception, was unaltered during the passage of the Bill through Parliament.*]

[C. T. Act, 1855.] 31. The Twenty-third Section of the principal Act shall extend to authorize a Compromise or Adjustment of any Claim, Demand, or Cause of Suit against any Charity, or the Trustees or Administrators thereof, and the Order of the Board in relation thereto shall have the like Effect as in the Case of any Compromise or Adjustment for which Provision is made by the said Section.

Extension of Power of Board as to Compromise of Claims.

[C. T. Act, 1853.] 27. Where any Land shall be required for the Erection or Construction of any House or Building with or without Garden, Playground or other Appurtenances, for the Purposes of any Charity, *and the Trustees of the Charity shall be legally authorized to purchase and hold such Land,*[*] but by reason of the Disability of any Person having an Estate or Interest in such Land, or of any Defect in Title thereto, a valid and perfect Assurance of the same Land cannot be made to the Trustees of the Charity in the ordinary Manner, it shall be lawful for the Trustees of the Charity, with the Sanction of the said Board (such Sanction to be certified under the Hand of their Secretary[†]), to take and purchase such Land according to the Provisions of "The Lands Clauses Consolidation Act, 1845;" and for that Purpose all the Clauses and Provisions of the last-mentioned Act with respect to the Purchase of Lands by Agreement, and with respect to the Purchase Money or Compensation coming to Parties having limited Interests, or prevented from treating, or not making a Title, and also with respect to Conveyances of Lands, so far as the same Clauses and Provisions respectively are applicable to the Cases contemplated by this Provision, shall be incorporated in this Act; and in all Cases contemplated by this Provision, the Expression "the Special Act" used in the said Clauses and Provisions of the said "Lands Clauses Consolidation Act" shall be construed to mean this Act; and the Expression "the Promoters of the Undertaking," used in the same Clauses and Provisions, shall be construed to mean the Trustees of the Charity in question.

Trustees of Charities enabled to purchase Sites for Building from Owners under Disability, &c. according to the Provisions of Lands Clauses Consolidation Act, 1845.

[C. T. Act, 1855.] 41. Section Twenty-seven of "The Charitable Trusts Act, 1853," shall be construed and operate as if the Words "and the Trustees of the Charity shall be legally authorized to purchase and hold such land" had been omitted therefrom; and incorporated Trustees of any Charity shall be competent to purchase and hold Lands for the Purposes mentioned in the same Section without Licence in Mortmain.

Construction of Sect. 27. of 16 & 17 Vict. c. 137.

[C. T. Act, 1855.] 32. The Board may authorize the Application of any Funds belonging to any Charity in Payments for Equality of Exchange or Partition,[‡] or in Payment of any Expenses incident thereto, or may authorize the Trustees to raise any Money for such Purposes by Mortgage of any Land acquired on such Exchange or Partition,[‡] or belonging to the Charity.

Board may authorize Payment for Equality of Exchange or Partition.

[C. T. Act, 1855.] 35. Any incorporated Charity, or the Trustees of any Charity, whether incorporated or not, may, with the Consent of the Board, invest Money arising from any Sale of Land belonging to the Charity, or received by way of Equality of Exchange or Partition,[‡] in the Purchase of Land, and may hold such Land, or any Land acquired by way of Exchange or Partition,[‡] for the Benefit of such Charity, without any Licence in Mortmain.

Incorporated Charities and Trustees for Charities may re-invest in Land.

[C. T. Act, 1860.] 15. The Power vested in the said Board by the Twenty-first Section of "The Charitable Trusts Act, 1853,"[§] of authorizing the Application of Monies belonging to any Charity or to be raised on the Security of the Properties thereof, to the Improvement of such Properties,

Sect. 21. of 16 & 17 Vict. c. 137. extended.

[* *Repealed by the Statute Law Revision Act, 1875 (38 & 39 Vict. c. 66).*]

[† *But see now Charitable Trusts Amendment Act, 1855, sect. 4 (p. 16), and Charitable Trusts Act, 1887, sect. 3 (p. 16).*]

[‡ *Neither this Act nor the Act of 1853 contains any section empowering the Commissioners to authorize partitions. Clauses numbered 39, 41, and 42 were introduced for that purpose into the Bill of 1855, as presented by the Lord Chancellor, but were struck out in Committee of the House of Commons. As regards Exchanges, see Charitable Trusts Act, 1853, sect. 21 (p. 29).*]

[§ *For this section see p. 27.*]

U 91117.　　　　　D

shall extend to authorize the Application of any like Monies to any other Purpose or Object which the Board shall consider to be beneficial to the Charity or the Estate or Objects thereof, and which shall not be inconsistent with the Trusts or Intentions of the Foundation.

Employment of persons to prepare and defend scheme.

[C. T. Act, 1869.] 9. The Board, if they think it desirable, where the gross annual income of a charity is in their opinion sufficient to bear the expense, may, upon the application of the trustees or of any other person or persons entitled to apply to them in that behalf, employ or may authorise the trustees or persons acting in the administration of such charity to employ skilled and competent persons to prepare any scheme, order, statement, or other proceeding for the purposes of the Charitable Trusts Acts, 1853 to 1869, with respect to such charity, or to make or assist in any survey or local inquiry with reference thereto, and may order the costs incurred under this section or upon any inquiry by an *inspector*,[*] or in consequence of the employment of any person to appear on behalf of the respondent upon any appeal against any scheme or order, to be provided in the same manner as if they were costs of a transaction mentioned in section thirty-six of the Charitable Trusts Act, 1855.[†]

VI.—Provisions conferring on the Charity Commissioners a control over dealings with the Real Estate of Charities, and facilitating those dealings.

Restrictions of Charges and Leases of Charity Estates.

[C. T. Act, 1855.] 29. It shall not be lawful for the Trustees or Persons acting in the Administration of any Charity to make or grant, otherwise than with the express Authority of Parliament, under any Act already passed or which may hereafter be passed, or of a Court or Judge of competent Jurisdiction, or according to a Scheme legally established, or with the Approval of the Board, any Sale, Mortgage, or Charge of the Charity Estate, or any Lease thereof in reversion after more than Three Years of any existing Term, or for any Term of Life, or in consideration wholly or in part of any Fine, or for any Term of Years exceeding Twenty-one Years.

[C. T. Act, 1862.] WHEREAS by the Acts relating to the Charity Commissioners for England and Wales, Authority has been given to the Commissioners to make Orders for various Purposes in Charity Cases upon summary Application, and particularly in relation to . . . . the Sale, Exchange, Leasing, and Improvement of the Property of Charities: And whereas in various Private Acts of Parliament and Decrees and Orders of the High Court of Chancery relating to Charities such Powers and Authorities are often given or reserved, with Directions that the same shall be exercised by the said Court, or with its Sanction or Approbation and Doubts are entertained whether in such Cases the Authority given to the Charity Commissioners can be validly exercised: Be it therefore enacted and declared *by the Queen's most Excellent Majesty, by and with the advice and consent of the Lords Spiritual and Temporal, and Commons, in this present Parliament assembled, and by the authority of the same*[‡] as follows:

No Provision in any Act of Parliament, or Decree relating to any Charity under any Order of the Court of Chancery, to exclude any Jurisdiction

1. No Provision contained in any such Act of Parliament or Decree or Order as aforesaid . . . . for or relating to the Sale, Exchange, Leasing, Disposal, or Improvement of any Property, by or under the Order or with the Approval of the Court of Chancery, shall (in the Absence of any express Direction to the contrary, to be contained in any future Act of Parliament,

[* Now "*Assistant Commissioner.*" *See the Charitable Trusts Act, 1887, sect. 2, sub-sect. 3 (p. 13).*]

[† *For this section see p. 29.*]

[‡ *Repealed by the Statute Law Revision Act, 1893 (56 Vict. c. 14.).*]

Order, or Decree,) exclude or impair any Jurisdiction or Authority which might otherwise be properly exercised for the like Purposes by the Charity Commissioners for England and Wales. *(margin: which might otherwise be exercised by the Charity Commissioners.)*

[*This section and the preamble are printed in full in Appendix, No. 1, p. 76.*]

[**C. T. Act, 1853.**] **21.** If in any Case it appear to the Trustees or Persons for the Time being acting in the Administration or Management of any Charity, or the Estates or Property thereof, that any part of the Charity Lands or Estates may be beneficially let on Building, Repairing, Improving, or other Leases, or on Leases for working any Mine, or that the digging for or raising of Stone, Clay, Gravel, or other Minerals, or the cutting of Timber, would be for the Benefit of the Charity, or that it would be for the Benefit of such Charity that any new Road or Street should be formed or laid out, or any Drains or Sewers made through any Part of the Charity Estates, or that any new Building should be erected, or that any existing Building should be repaired, altered, rebuilt, or wholly removed, or that any other Improvements or Alterations in the State or Condition of the Lands or Estates of such Charity should be made, it shall be lawful for such Trustees or Persons to lay before the said Board a Statement and Proposal in relation to any of the Matters aforesaid; and it shall be lawful for the said Board, if they think that the Leases or Acts to which the Statement and Proposal relate (with or without Modifications or Alterations) would be beneficial to the Charity, to make such Order under their Seal for and in relation to the granting of such Leases, or the doing of any other such Acts as aforesaid, and any Circumstances connected therewith, as they may think fit, although such Leases or Acts respectively shall not be authorized or permitted by the Trust; and the said Board, by any such Order, may authorize the Application of any Monies or Funds belonging to the Charity for any of the Purposes or Acts aforesaid, and, if necessary, may authorize the Trustees to raise any Sum of Money by Mortgage of all or any Part of the Charity Estates; *provided that compulsory Provisions be reserved in every such Mortgage for the Payment of the Principal Money borrowed by annual Instalments, and for the Redemption and Re-conveyance of the mortgaged Estates, within the Period of not more than Thirty Years.* *(margin: Board may sanction Building Leases, working Mines, doing Repairs and Improvements; and may authorize the Application of the Charity Funds or the raising of Money on Mortgage for those Purposes.)*

[**C. T. Act, 1855.**] **30.** *So much of Section Twenty-one of the principal Act as requires a compulsory Provision to be inserted in every Mortgage for the Payment of the Principal Money borrowed by annual Instalments, and for the Redemption and Reconveyance of the mortgaged Estates within the Period of not more than Thirty Years, is hereby repealed; but** the Board authorizing any Mortgage to be made of any Charity Estate shall make such Provisions, by the same or any other Order, as to them may seem necessary, for directing the Trustees or Persons administering the Charity to discharge the Principal Debt or any Part thereof by such yearly or other Instalments within Thirty Years from the Date of the Security as to the said Board may seem fit; or to form an Accumulation or Sinking Fund out of the Income of the Charity for discharging the Principal Debt or any Portion thereof within the same Period, and shall give Directions as to the Investment and Accumulation of such Fund, and the Trustees for the Time being, or Persons administering the Charity, shall carry such Order into effect. *(margin: Sinking Fund to be provided for paying off Mortgages in lieu of Provision in Mortgage Deeds.)*

[**C. T. Act, 1860.**] **15.** The Power vested in the said Board by the Twenty-first Section of "The Charitable Trusts Act, 1853," of authorizing the Application of Monies belonging to any Charity or to be raised on the Security of the Properties thereof, to the Improvement of such Properties, shall extend to authorize the Application of any like Monies to any other Purpose or Object which the Board shall consider to be beneficial to the Charity or the Estate or Objects thereof, and which shall not be inconsistent with the Trusts or Intentions of the Foundation. *(margin: Sect. 21 of 16 & 17 Vict. c. 137, extended.)*

[* *Repealed by the Statute Law Revision Act, 1875 (38 & 39 Vict. c. 66).*]

D 2

Board may approve Schemes for letting Charitable Property.

[C. T. Act, 1855.] 39. It shall be lawful for the Board to prepare, and under their seal to approve of, any Scheme for the letting of the Property or any Part of the Property of any Charity; and all Leases granted by any Trustees or Persons acting in the Management of any Charity, pursuant to or in conformity with such Scheme, shall be valid.

Board, under special Circumstances, may authorise Sale or Exchange of Charity Lands.

C. T. Act, 1853.] 24. Upon Application to the said Board by the Trustees or Persons acting in the Administration of any Charity, representing to the said Board that, under the special Circumstances of any Land belonging to the Charity, a Sale or Exchange of such Land can be effected on such Terms as to increase the Income of the Charity, or would otherwise be advantageous to the Charity, such Board may, if they think fit, inquire into such Circumstances, and if after Inquiry they are satisfied that the proposed Sale or Exchange will be advantageous to the Charity may authorize the Sale or Exchange, and give such Directions in relation thereto, and for securing the due Investment of the Money arising from any such Sale, or by way of Equality of Exchange for the Benefit of the Charity, as they may think fit.

Board may authorize the Redemption of Rent-charges.

C. T. Act, 1853.] 25. The said Board shall have Authority, upon such Application as aforesaid, to authorize the Sale to the Owners of the Land charged therewith of any Rentcharge, Annuity, or other periodical Payment charged upon Land and payable to or for the Benefit of any Charity, or applicable to Charitable Purposes, upon such Terms and Conditions as they may deem beneficial to the Charity, and to give such Directions for securing the due Investment of the Money arising from such Sale for the Benefit of the Charity, or for securing the due Application thereof to such Charitable Purposes, as they may think fit; and in like Manner the Trustees of any Charity, with the Consent of the Board, may purchase any Rentcharge or other yearly Payment to which the Charity Estate is or shall be liable.

Leases, Sales, &c. authorized by the Board to be valid.

[C. T. Act, 1853.] 26. The Leases, Sales, Exchanges, and other Transactions authorized by such Board under the Powers of this Act shall have the like Effect and Validity as if they had been authorized or directed by the express Terms of the Trust affecting the Charity.

Leases, &c. to be valid, notwithstanding disabling Acts.

[C. T. Act, 1855.] 38. All Leases. Sales, Exchanges, Partitions,* and Transactions authorized by the Board under the principal Act† or this Act shall be valid and effectual, notwithstanding the Act of the Thirteenth Year of the Reign of Queen Elizabeth, Chapter Ten, the Acts of the Fourteenth Year of the same Queen, Chapters Eleven and Fourteen, the Acts of the Eighteenth Year of the same Queen, Chapters Six and Eleven, the Act of the Thirty-ninth Year of the same Queen, Chapter Five, and the Act of the Twenty-first year of the Reign of King James the First, Chapter One, or any disabling Act applicable to the Charity the Estates whereof shall be the Subject of any such Transaction.

Board may authorize Payment for Equality of Exchange or Partition.

[C. T. Act, 1855.] 32. The Board may authorize the Application of any Funds belonging to any Charity in Payments for Equality of Exchange or Partition,* or in Payment of any Expenses incident thereto, or may authorize the Trustees to raise any Money for such Purposes by Mortgage of any Land acquired on such Exchange or Partition,* or belonging to the Charity.

Expenses of Exchanges and Partitions, and determining Application of Charges.

[C. T. Act, 1855.] 34. The Expenses incidental to the Application for and procuring of any such Order of Exchange or Partition* . . . . shall be paid by the Trustees or Administrators of the Charity, or by the other Parties to such Transactions, or by both, as the Board may direct.

[*This section is printed in full in Appendix, No. 1, p. 74.*]

_____

Neither this Act, nor the Act of 1853 contains any section empowering the Commissioners to authorise partitions. Clauses numbered 39, 41, and 42 were introduced for that purpose into the Bill of 1855, as presented by the Lord Chancellor, but were struck out in Committee of the House of Commons.]

[† *i.e., the Charitable Trusts Act,* 1853.]

[C. T. Act, 1855.] 35. Any incorporated Charity, or the Trustees of any Charity, whether incorporated or not, may, with the Consent of the Board, invest Money arising from any Sale of Land belonging to the Charity, or received by way of Equality of Exchange or Partition,* in the Purchase of Land, and may hold such Land, or any Land acquired by way of Exchange or Partition,* for the Benefit of such Charity, without any Licence in Mortmain.

Incorporated Charities and Trustees for Charities may re-invest in Land.

[C. T. Act, 1855.] 36. All Orders of the Board for the Investment of Money coming to any Charity or the Trustees thereof on any Sale, Exchange, or Partition* shall be carried into effect by the Trustees or Persons administering the Charity; and all Monies which the Board shall order to be provided out of any Income or Property of a Charity for the Payment of the Costs of any such Transaction shall be provided or raised by the Trustees or Administrators of the Charity, and applied accordingly.

Order of Board for Investments to be carried into effect, and Cost to be raised.

[C. T. Act, 1855.] 37. It shall be lawful for the Board to authorize or order and direct the Official Trustee of Charity Lands . . . . to convey Lands, ... as the Board shall think expedient.

[*This section is printed in full in Appendix, No. 1. p. 74.*]

Board may direct Official Trustees to convey Lands, &c.

[C. T. Act, 1855.] 16. The acting Trustees of every Charity, or the Majority of them, provided that such Majority do not consist of less than Three Persons, shall have at Law and in Equity Power to grant all such Leases or Tenancies of Land belonging thereto, and vested in the Official Trustee of Charity Lands, as they would have Power to grant in the due Administration of the Charity if the same Land were legally vested in themselves; and all Covenants, Conditions, and Remedies contained in or incident to any Lease or Tenancy so granted shall be enforceable by and against the Trustees or Persons acting in the Administration of the Charity for the Time being, and their Alienees or Assigns, in like Manner as if such Lands had been legally vested in the Trustees granting such Lease or Tenancy at the Time of the Execution thereof, and had legally remained in or had devolved to such Trustees or Administrators for the Time being, their Alienees or Assigns, subject to the same Lease or Tenancy.

Power to acting Trustees to grant Leases.

[C. T. Act, 1860.] 16. *A Majority of Two Thirds of the Trustees of any Charity assembled at a Meeting of their Body duly constituted, and having Power to determine on any Sale, Exchange, Partition, Mortgage, Lease, or other Disposition of any Property of the Charity, shall also have a legal Power, on behalf of themselves and their Co-trustees, and also of the Official Trustee of Charity Lands, where his Concurrence would be otherwise required, to do, enter into, and execute all such Acts, Deeds, Contracts, and Assurances as shall be requisite for carrying any such Sale, Exchange, Partition, Mortgage, Lease, or Disposition into legal Effect, and all such Acts, Deeds, Contracts, or Assurances shall have the same legal Effect as if the same were respectively done, entered into, or executed by all the acting Trustees for the Time being, and by the said Official Trustee.†*

A Majority of Trustees to have legal Power of dealing with the Charity Estates.

[C. T. Act, 1869.] 12. Where the trustees or persons acting in the administration of any charity have power to determine on any sale, exchange, partition, mortgage, lease, or other disposition of any property of the charity, a majority of those trustees or persons who are present at a meeting of their body duly constituted and vote on the question shall have and be deemed to have always had full power to execute and do all such assurances, acts, and things as may be requisite for carrying any such sale, exchange, partition, mortgage, lease, or disposition into effect, and all such assurances, acts, and things shall have the same effect as if they were respectively executed and done by all such trustees or persons for the time being and by the official trustee of charity lands.

Legal power of majority of trustees to deal with Charity estates.

[* *Neither this Act, nor the Act of 1853 contains any section empowering the Commissioners to authorise partitions. Clauses numbered 30, 31, and 12 were introduced for that purpose into the Bill of 1855, as presented by the Lord Chancellor, but were struck out in Committee of the House of Commons.*]

[† *Repealed by Charitable Trusts Act, 1869, sect. 17 (p. 72)*]

VII.—Provisions as to the Preservation of Charity Property by means of—

(1.) *THE OFFICIAL TRUSTEE OF CHARITY LANDS;*

(2.) *THE OFFICIAL TRUSTEES OF CHARITABLE FUNDS;*

(3.) *THE VESTING OR TRANSFER OF PROPERTY OTHER-WISE THAN BY ORDER OF A COURT OR JUDGE;*

(4.) *THE DEPOSIT FOR SAFE CUSTODY AND THE ENROL-MENT OF DEEDS, WILLS, OR DOCUMENTS;*

(5.) *THE EXEMPTION FROM INCOME TAX OF DIVIDENDS UPON STOCK IN THE PUBLIC FUNDS.*

(6.) *THE TAXATION OF BILLS OF COSTS.*

(1.) *THE OFFICIAL TRUSTEE OF CHARITY LANDS.*

(a.) *Constitution of the Official Trustee of Charity Lands.*

Secretary to be Treasurer of Charities; such Treasurer to be a Corporation. [**C. T. Act, 1853.**] **47.** The Secretary for the Time being of the said Board shall by virtue of his Appointment be the *Treasurer of Public Charities;* and such Treasurer shall for the Purposes of taking, holding, conveying, assigning, transferring, and transmitting Real Property, including Leaseholds for Lives or Years, be a Corporation Sole by the Name of " *The Treasurer of Public Charities,*" and by that Name shall have perpetual Succession, and plead and be impleaded before all Courts, Justices, and others.

The Official Trustee of Charity Lands constituted. [**C. T. Act, 1855.**] **15.** The Secretary for the Time being of the Board shall be a Corporation Sole by the Name of " The Official Trustee of Charity Lands," for taking and holding Charity Lands, and by that Name (instead of the Name of " Treasurer of Public Charities ") shall have perpetual Succession ; and all Land, or Estates or Interests in Land, now vested in the " Treasurer of Public Charities " by that Name shall become, upon the passing of this Act, and by virtue thereof, vested in like Manner and upon the same Trusts in " The Official Trustee of Charity Lands," and all Provisions of the principal Act which have reference to the Treasurer of Public Charities shall operate as if the Name of the " Official Trustee of Charity Lands " had been used therein instead of the Name of " Treasurer of Public Charities."

Declaration as to power of official trustee of charity lands to take and hold land. [**C. T. Act, 1887.**] **5.** The official trustee of charity lands shall be authorised and be deemed always to have been authorised to take and hold all such land and estate or interest in land, as, in pursuance of an order of the Board, is conveyed to or vested in him by any deed or assurance or otherwise.

(b.) *Vesting Land in the Official Trustee of Charity Lands.*

Land holden upon trust for a Charity, subject to Jurisdiction of Court of Chancery and of Judge, may be vested in Treasurer. [**C. T. Act, 1853.**] **48.** Where any Land, or any Term or Estate therein, holden upon trust for any Charity, shall be vested in any Persons other than the Persons acting in the Administration and Application of the Rents; or where there shall be no Trustees thereof, or the Trustees, or any of them, shall be unwilling to act, or it shall be uncertain in whom such Land, Term or Estate, shall be vested, or all, or any of the Persons in whom such Land, Term or Estate, shall be vested, cannot be found, or shall be under Age, lunatic, or of unsound mind, (whether found such by Inquisition or not,) or otherwise incapable of acting, or shall be out of the Jurisdiction or not amenable to the Process of the Court of Chancery, or where by reason of the reduced Number of Trustees or other Causes a valid Appointment of new Trustees cannot be made, or where by reason of the Expenses incident to the Appointment of new Trustees, and the Conveyance or Assignment of such Land, Term or Estate, to such new Trustees, it shall appear to the Court of Chancery, or to any Judge of such Court or of any Court having Jurisdiction with respect to such Charity under this Act,* desirable so to do, such Court or Judge may Order that such Land, Term or Estate, be vested in such *Treasurer*,† and thereupon the same shall vest in such *Treasurer*† and his Successors for all the Estate and Interest holden in trust for the Charity as aforesaid, without any Conveyance or Assurance thereof ; but no such Vesting Order as aforesaid, shall be made in respect of any Land, or Term or Estate as aforesaid, holden in Trust as aforesaid, vested in a Corporation, without the Consent of the Corporation ; and no such Vesting Order shall take effect in respect of any Copyhold Land without the Consent of the Lord of the Manor ; and the Court of Chancery, or such Judge, may direct such periodical or other Payment, as such Court or Judge may think fit, to be made to the Lord of the Manor, in compensation for Fines or other Profits which would have become due upon Death or Admittance of Tenants. Proviso.

[**Local Government Act, 1894 (56 & 57 Vict. c. 73).**] **52. (4.**) Where the legal estate in any property is vested in the churchwardens and overseers of any parish by virtue of the Poor Relief Act, 1819. nothing in the Charitable Trusts Acts, 1853 to 1891, shall be deemed to require the consent of such churchwardens and overseers in their capacity as a corporation under that Act, or of the parish council as their successors, to a vesting order under those Acts dealing with the said legal estate. Provided that nothing in this section shall affect any rights, powers, or duties of the churchwardens and overseers or the parish council, in cases where they have active powers of management.

[**C. T. Act, 1853.**] **49.** It shall be lawful for any Court or Judge by whom respectively any such Vesting Order may have been made, or for any other Court or Judge having Jurisdiction in the Matter, if it shall so seem fit to such Court or Judge, from Time to Time to order that all or any Part of the Land, Term or Estate, which shall for the Time being be vested in the said *Treasurer*† by virtue of any such Vesting Order as aforesaid, shall be devested, and that the same shall be vested in the acting Trustee or Trustees for the Time being of the Charity ; and such last-mentioned Order shall operate to vest such Land, Term and Estate, in the Trustees or Trustee therein named without any Conveyance or Assurance. Orders may be made revesting Land, &c, in the Trustees of the Charity.

[**C. T. Act, 1860.**] **2.** The Board of Charity Commissioners for England and Wales, subject to the Restrictions and Rights of Appeal hereinafter provided, shall have Power from Time to Time, upon the Application of any Person or Persons who, under the Forty-third Section of "The Charitable Trusts Act, 1853, might be authorized to apply to any Judge or Court for the like Purposes, to make such effectual Orders as may now be made by any Judge of the Court of Chancery sitting at Chambers, or by any County Court *or District Court of Bankruptcy* ‡ [for the appointment or removal of Trustees of any Charity . . . . or] for or relating to the . . . . vesting of any Real . . . Estate belonging thereto,§ . . . . Certain administrative Powers to be exercisable by the Charity Commissioners.

[This section is printed in full in Appendix, No. 1, p. 75.]

(c.) *Conditions of Trusteeship of the Official Trustee of Charity Lands.*

[**C. T. Act, 1855.**] **37.** It shall be lawful for the Board to authorize or order and direct the Official Trustee of Charity Lands . . . . to convey Lands . . . . as the Board shall think expedient. Board may direct Official Trustee to convey Land, &c.

[This section is printed in full in Appendix, No. 1, p. 74.]

[* *For the jurisdiction under the Charitable Trusts Acts* (1) *of a Judge of the Chancery Division of the High Court of Justice at Chambers, see p.* 64: (2) *of the Chancery Court of the County Palatine of Lancaster, see p.* 64 : *and* (3) *of the County Courts, see p.* 65.]
[† *Now "The Official Trustee of Charity Lands."*]
[‡ *Repealed by the Statute Law Revision Act, 1875* (38 & 39 *Vict. c.* 66.)]
[§ *For the provisions of the Charitable Trusts Acts, which regulate the exercise by the Charity Commissioners of their jurisdiction under this section to make vesting orders, see p.* 38.]

Treasurer to be a Bare Trustee.

[**C. T. Act, 1853.**] **50.** Subject to the Orders and Directions of the Court of Chancery or of any such Judge,* such Treasurer† shall be deemed a Bare Trustee, and shall permit the Persons acting in the Administration of the Charity to have the Possession, Management, and Control of the Trust Estates, and the Application of the Income thereof, as if the same had been vested in them.

Power to acting Trustees to grant Leases.

[**C. T. Act, 1855.**] **16.** The Acting Trustees of every Charity, or the Majority of them, provided that such Majority do not consist of less than Three Persons, shall have at Law and in Equity Power to grant all such Leases or Tenancies of Land belonging thereto, and vested in the Official Trustee of Charity Lands, as they would have Power to grant in the due Administration of the Charity if the same Land were legally vested in themselves; and all Covenants, Conditions, and Remedies contained in or incident to any Lease or Tenancy so granted shall be enforceable by and against the Trustees or Persons acting in the Administration of the Charity for the Time being, and their Alienees or Assigns, in like Manner as if such Lands had been legally vested in the Trustees granting such Lease or Tenancy at the Time of the Execution thereof, and had legally remained in or had devolved to such Trustees or Administrators for the Time being, their Alienees or Assigns, subject to the same Lease or Tenancy.

A Majority of Trustees to have legal Power of dealing with the Charity Estates.

[**C. T. Act, 1860.**] **16.** *A Majority of Two Thirds of the Trustees of any Charity assembled at a Meeting of their Body duly constituted, and having Power to determine on any Sale, Exchange, Partition, Mortgage, Lease, or other Disposition of any Property of the Charity, shall also have a legal Power, on behalf of themselves and their Co-trustees, and also of the Official Trustee of Charity Lands, where his Concurrence would be otherwise required, to do, enter into, and execute all such Acts, Deeds, Contracts, and Assurances as shall be requisite for carrying any such Sale, Exchange, Partition, Mortgage, Lease, or Disposition into legal Effect, and all such Acts, Deeds, Contracts, or Assurances shall have the same legal Effect as if the same were respectively done, entered into, or executed by all the acting Trustees for the Time being, and by the said Official Trustee.‡*

Legal power of majority of Trustees to deal with charity estates.

[**C. T. Act, 1869.**] **12.** Where the trustees or persons acting in the administration of any charity have power to determine on any sale, exchange, partition, mortgage, lease, or other disposition of any property of the charity, a majority of those trustees or persons who are present at a meeting of their body duly constituted and vote on the question shall have and be deemed to have always had full power to execute and do all such assurances, acts, and things as may be requisite for carrying any such sale, exchange, partition, mortgage, lease, or disposition into effect, and all such assurances, acts, and things shall have the same effect as if they were respectively executed and done by all such trustees or persons for the time being and by the official trustee of charity lands.

(2.) *THE OFFICIAL TRUSTEES OF CHARITABLE FUNDS.*

(a.) *Constitution of the Official Trustees.*

Judge may order Trustee, &c. holding Stock, &c. belonging to a Charity subject to his Jurisdiction to transfer same to Official Trustees.

[**C. T. Act, 1853.**] **51.** *The Secretary for the Time being of the said Board, and such other public Officer or Officers as the Lord Chancellor shall appoint, shall be official Trustees of Charitable Funds,§* . . . .

[*This section is printed in full in Appendix, No. 1, p. 74.*]

Appointments of Official Trustees of Charitable Funds regulated.

[**C. T. Act, 1855.**] **17.** *The Lord Chancellor may from Time to Time by Writing under his Hand appoint any Persons to be, jointly with the Secretary for the Time being of the said Board, the Official Trustees of Charitable Funds, and remove any such Trustees, and every such Appointment or Removal shall be published in the London Gazette.§*

---

* *See section 49 of the Charitable Trusts Act, 1853 (p. 31).*]
† *Now " The Official Trustee of Charity Lands."*]
‡ *Repealed by the Charitable Trusts Act, 1869, sect. 17 (p. 72).*]
§ *Repealed by the Charitable Trusts Act, 1887, sect. 6 (p. 72).*]

[C. T. Act, 1855.] 18. The *present* Official Trustees of Charitable Funds, and their Successors, *to be so appointed,* shall have perpetual Succession by the Name of "The Official Trustees of Charitable Funds," and may hold by that Name Stock in the Public Funds, and Stock and Shares of any Public Company, Securities, and Monies, which shall respectively devolve to their Successors, the Official Trustees of Charitable Funds for the Time being, without Transfer or Assignment.

Such Trustees to have perpetual Succession, and may hold Funds in that Name.

[C. T. Act, 1855.] 19. *All Stock in the Public Funds vested in the joint Names of Henry Morgan Vane, Thomas Hare, and Walker Skirrow, Esquires, the present Official Trustees of Charitable Funds, shall upon the passing of this Act be transferred by the Governor and Company of the Bank of England from their Names to the Account of the Official Trustees of Charitable Funds.†*

Funds to vest in the Official Trustees for the Time being.

[C. T. Act, 1887.] 4.—(1.) From and after the date fixed by a regulation under this section,‡ such officers of the Board as the Board with the approval of the Treasury from time to time appoint shall, in lieu of the persons mentioned in the Charitable Trusts Amendment Act, 1855, be the official trustees of charitable funds:

Provided that any inspector or officer of the Board, who at the passing of this Act is official trustee of charitable funds, and is not, after the passing of this Act, appointed to be official trustee shall, while he continues to hold his inspectorship or office, receive not less salary than he received while official trustee. . . . .

Amendment of Charitable Trusts Acts as to official trustees of charitable funds.

[*This section is printed in full in Appendix, No. 1, p. 76.*]

(b.) Statutory Indemnity to the Official Trustees.

[C. T. Act, 1860.] 17. No Official Trustee of Charitable Funds, *appointed under or in pursuance of the first or secondly recited Act*,§ shall be chargeable with or accountable for any Loss or Misapplication of the said Charitable Funds, or the Dividends, Interest, or Income thereof, unless the same shall have been occasioned by or through his own wilful Neglect or Default.

Official Trustee not to be accountable for Loss unless occasioned by his own Neglect.

(c.) Provisions authorizing Transfers and Payments to the Official Trustees.

[C. T. Act, 1853.] 51. . . . . Where Trustees or other Persons having in their Names, or in the Name of any deceased Person of whom they are Representatives, in the Books of the Bank of England, or of the East India or South Sea Company, or of any other public Company, any Annuities, Stock or Shares, or holding any Government or Parliamentary or other Securities in trust for any Charity, shall be desirous to transfer or deposit the same to or with the said official Trustees in trust for such Charity, or where any Persons shall be desirous of transferring or depositing as aforesaid any Annuities, Stocks, Shares, or Securities, for discharging any Legacy or Charge given or made to or for the Benefit of any Charity, or where it shall appear to the Court of Chancery, or to any Judge of such Court, or of any *District Court of Bankruptcy, or‖* County Court having Jurisdiction under this Act,¶ that any Annuities, Stock, Shares, or Securities, held in trust for any Charity ought, for the Purpose of Security or convenient Administration, to be transferred or deposited as aforesaid, it shall be lawful for such Court or Judge to order the Transfer or Deposit of such Annuities, Stock, Shares, or Securities to or with such official Trustees.

[*This section is printed in full in Appendix, No. 1, p. 74.*]

[* Repealed by the Charitable Trusts Act, 1887, sect. 6 (p. 72).]
[† Repealed by the Statute Law Revision Act, 1875 (38 & 39 Vict. c. 66.).]
[‡ 1st April 1889. See Treasury Regulations of 27th March 1889, clause 1 (p. 36) ;
[§ Repealed by the Charitable Trusts Act, 1887, sect. 6 (p. 72).]
[‖ Repealed by the Statute Law Revision Act, 1892 (55 & 56 Vict. c. 19.).]
[¶ For the jurisdiction under the Charitable Trusts Acts (1) of a Judge of the Chancery Division of the High Court of Justice at Chambers, see p. 61 ; (2) of the Chancery Court of the County Palatine of Lancaster, see p. 61; and (3) of the County Courts, see p. 65 ;

The Official Trustees of Charitable Funds may be empowered to call for Transfers to them of Stock, &c.

[C. T. Act, 1855.] 12. Any Court or Judge having Jurisdiction to order the Transfer of Stock in the Public Funds, or Stock or Shares of any public Company, to the Official Trustees of Charitable Funds, shall have Power also to authorize such Trustees to call for a Transfer of and to transfer such Stock or Shares, and may also order the Payment to the same Trustees of any Principal Monies of any Charity, under the same Circumstances in which the Transfer of Stock to them may now be ordered.

Trustees may transfer Stock to Official Trustees.

[C. T. Act, 1855.] 22. Any Trustee or other Person may, on obtaining an Order of the Board for the Purpose, transfer any Stock or pay any Money to the Official Trustees of Charitable Funds in trust for any Charity.

Certain administrative Powers to be exercisable by the Charity Commissioners.

[C. T. Act, 1860.] 2. The Board of Charity Commissioners for England and Wales, subject to the Restrictions and Rights of Appeal herein-after provided, shall have Power from Time to Time, upon the Application of any Person or Persons who, under the Forty-third Section of "The Charitable Trusts Act, 1853," might be authorized to apply to any Judge or Court for the like Purposes, to make such effectual Orders as may now be made by any Judge of the Court of Chancery sitting at Chambers, or by any County Court *or District Court of Bankruptcy,* [for the appointment or removal of Trustees of any Charity . . . . or] for or relating to the Assurance, Transfer, Payment, or vesting of any . . . . Personal Estate belonging thereto, or entitling the Official Trustees of Charitable Funds . . . . . to call for a Transfer of and to transfer any Stock belonging to such Estate† . . . .

[*This section is printed in full in Appendix, No.* 1, *p.* 75.]

Official Trustees of Charitable Funds may be empowered to receive Arrears of Dividends.

[C. T. Act, 1860.] 12. Any Court or Judge, or the said Board, having Jurisdiction to authorize the Official Trustees of Charitable Funds to call for a Transfer of and to transfer any Annuities, Stock, or Securities, may empower them also to receive and recover, in trust for the Charity to which the same shall belong, all Dividends, Interest, and Income accrued from any such Annuities, Stock, or Securities respectively, and which shall for the Time being be in arrear.

(*d.*) *Functions of the Official Trustees, and Provisions regulating the Mode in which the Business of the Official Trustees generally is to be conducted.*

Secretary to keep separate Accounts of Funds of each Charity.

[C. T. Act, 1853.] 52. *The Secretary of the said Board shall keep separate Accounts of the Annuities, Stock, Shares, and Securities belonging to each separate Charity, and*‡ the said official Trustees shall pay the Dividends or Interest or Income thereof to the Trustees or Persons acting in the Administration of such Charity, or otherwise dispose thereof, and transfer such Annuities, Stock, Shares, or Securities (when Occasion shall require), as the Court of Chancery, or any Judge of such Court, or of any *District Court of Bankruptcy, or*§ County Court having Jurisdiction under this Act,‖ or other lawful Authority, shall direct.

Board may direct Official Trustees to convey Lands, &c.

[C. T. Act, 1855.] 37. It shall be lawful for the Board to authorize or order and direct . . . . the Official Trustees of Charitable Funds . . . . to assign, transfer, and pay over Stocks, Funds, Monies, and Securities, as the Board shall think expedient.

[*This section is printed in full in Appendix, No.* 1, *p.* 74.]

[* *Repealed by the Statute Law Revision Act,* 1875 (38 & 39 Vict. c. 66.).]
[† *For the provisions of the Charitable Trusts Acts, which regulate the exercise by the Charity Commissioners of their jurisdiction under this section to make orders for the transfer, &c. of personal estate belonging to Charities, see p.* 38.]
[‡ *Repealed by the Charitable Trusts Act,* 1887, *sect.* 6 (*p.* 72).]
[§ *Repealed by the Statute Law Revision Act,* 1892 (55 & 56 Vict. c. 19.).]
[‖ *See footnote* * *on preceding page.*]

[C. T. Act, 1855.] 20. The Official Trustees of Charitable Funds shall, for the Purposes of their Trust, keep a Banking Account in their official Name in the Books of *the Governor and Company of* * the Bank of England, *and the Secretary of the Board shall keep separate Accounts of the Monies held upon such Account, and belonging to each separate Charity.*† — The Official Trustees to keep Banking Account.

[C. T. Act, 1855.] 23. All Principal Monies belonging to any Charity directed to be paid to the Official Trustees of Charitable Funds shall be paid to their Account at the Bank, and, subject to any Order of the Court or Judge or of the Board by which respectively the Payment shall have been authorized, shall be forthwith invested in the Public Funds, in the Names of the Official Trustees of Charitable Funds, for the Benefit of the Charity to which they shall belong. — As to Disposal of Principal Monies paid to them.

[C. T. Act, 1855.] 24. The Dividends arising from all Stock in the Public Funds standing in the Name of the Official Trustees of Charitable Funds shall from Time to Time be received by *the Governor and Company of* * the Bank of England, under the Authority of this Act, for the Credit of the said Official Trustees, and shall be placed to their Banking Account accordingly; and all Dividends and Interest arising from any other Stock, Shares, or Securities standing in the Name of or held by the Official Trustees of Charitable Funds shall be paid only to *the Governor and Company of* * the Bank of England for the Account of the same Trustees; *and the said Trustees shall from Time to Time execute to the said Governor and Company all such Powers as shall be found necessary for enabling them to receive and give effectual Discharges for the last-mentioned Dividends and Interest.*† — All Dividends and Interest due to the Official Trustees of Charitable Funds to be placed to their Banking Account.

[C. T. Act, 1855.] 21. All Orders for Payment of any Money held upon such Banking Account shall be signed by One at least of the Official Trustees of Charitable Funds, not being the Secretary of the Board, and also by the Secretary, and shall be countersigned by One of the Commissioners, or shall be otherwise signed or authenticated in such Manner as the Lord Chancellor shall from Time to Time by Order under his Hand direct; and such Orders shall be a sufficient Authority to the Bank paying the same for all such Payments.‡ — Mode of drawing on the Banking Account.

[C. T. Act, 1855.] 25. No Transfer of any Stock, Shares, or Securities shall be made to the Official Trustees of Charitable Funds, nor shall any Money, other than the Dividends or Interest of any such Stock, Shares, or Securities as aforesaid, be paid to their Account, except in pursuance of an Order of the Court of Chancery, or of some Judge thereof, or of a *District Court of Bankruptcy or* § County Court, or of the Board; and no Transfer of any such Stock, Shares, or Securities shall be made by the Official Trustees, except under the Order of such Court or Judge, or under the Order of the Board signed by Two Commissioners, or authenticated in such Manner as the Lord Chancellor from Time to Time by any Order under his Hand direct;‖ and no Transfer to or by the Official Trustees shall be permitted by *the Governor and Company of* * the Bank of England or any other Company contrary to this Provision. — For the Regulation of Transfers and Payments to or by the Official Trustees.

[C. T. Act, 1855.] 26. Copies of all Orders made by any Court or Judge for any Transfer, Deposit, or Payment of Stock, Shares, Securities, or Monies to or by the Official Trustees of Charitable Funds shall be forthwith transmitted to the Board by the Parties obtaining such Orders. — Copies of Orders affecting the Account of the Official Trustees to be sent to the Board.

[* *Repealed by the Statute Law Revision Act, 1892 (55 & 56 Vict. c. 19.).*]
[† *Repealed by the Charitable Trusts Act, 1887, sect. 6 (p. 72).*]
[‡ *But see now the Charitable Trusts Act, 1887, sect. 1, sub-sects. 2 (b.) and 4 (p. 36), and Treasury Regulations of 27th March 1889, clause 4 (p. 37).*]
[§ *Repealed by the Statute Law Revision Act, 1875 (38 & 39 Vict. c. 66.).*]
[‖ *But see now the Charitable Trusts Act, 1887, sect. 1, sub-sects. 2 (b.) and 4 (p. 36), and Treasury Regulations of 27th March 1889, clauses 4 and 9 (p. 37).*]

Indemnity to the Bank and others

[**C. T. Act, 1855.**] 27. Every Order made under the principal Act or this Act, requiring or authorizing the Transfer, Payment, or Deposit of any Stock, Shares, Securities, or Monies to or with [the Trustees of any Charity or] the Official Trustees of Charitable Funds, or conferring a Right to call for or to make such Transfer, shall be a complete Indemnity to the Governor and Company of the Bank of England and all Companies and Persons for any Act done pursuant to such Order; and the said Governor and Company and other Companies and Persons shall be required to give effect or to conform to every such Order, and it shall not be necessary for them to inquire concerning the Propriety of such Order, or the Jurisdiction of the Court or Judge or the Board to make the same.

Indemnity to the Bank of England and others.

[**C. T. Act, 1860.**] 23. Every Order made under this Act under which any Stock, Shares, Securities, or Monies shall be transferred or paid to or deposited with [the Trustees of any Charity, or] the Official Trustees of Charitable Funds, shall afford a complete Indemnity to the Governor and Company of the Bank of England, and to all Companies and Persons by whom respectively any such Transfer, Payment, or Deposit shall be permitted or made, for permitting or making the same, and the said Governor and Company and other Companies and Persons shall be required to give effect or to conform to such Order, and it shall not be necessary for them to inquire concerning the Propriety of the same Order, or the Jurisdiction under which the same shall purport to be made.

Amendment of Charitable Trusts Acts as to official trustees of charitable funds.

[**C. T. Act, 1887.**] 4.—(1.) . . . .
(2.) From and after the said date,* notwithstanding anything in the Charitable Trusts Acts, 1853 to 1869, the Treasury may, by regulations to be made or approved by them,† from time to time prescribe :

(*a*) the accounts to be kept by the said official trustees and the mode in which and the persons by whom such accounts and the banking accounts, and any other accounts required by the Charitable Trusts Acts, 1853 to 1869, to be kept by or on behalf of the official trustees of charitable funds, are to be kept ;

(*b*) the mode in which orders authorised by law for the payment of any money to or by the said official trustees or held upon their banking account, or for the transfer of any stock or securities to or by the said official trustees, are to be signed, authenticated, and carried into effect ; and

(*c*) the mode in which the business of the said official trustees generally is to be conducted :

Provided that separate accounts shall continue to be kept for each charity.
(3.) The accounts of the said official trustees shall be audited by such person and in accordance with such regulations as the Treasury from time to time appoint or prescribe.
(4.) A regulation under this section, or an order made under any such regulation, shall be a complete indemnity to the Governor and Company of the Bank of England, and all companies and persons, for any act done pursuant to such regulation or order, and the said Governor and Company, and other Companies and persons, shall conform to such regulation or order.

[*This section is printed in full in Appendix, No. 1, p. 76.*]

OFFICIAL TRUSTEES OF CHARITABLE FUNDS (TREASURY REGULATIONS).

Regulations made by the Treasury under Section 4 of the Charitable Trusts Act, 1887 (50 & 51 Vict. c. 49).

1. These regulations shall take effect on and from 1st April 1889; and that date is hereby fixed as the date from and after which such officers of the Charity Commission as the Charity Commissioners, with the approval of the Treasury, shall have appointed,

[* 1st April 1889. *See Treasury Regulations of 27th March 1889, cl. 1. infra.*]
[† *See infra.*]

or shall appoint for that purpose, under section 4 (1) of the Charitable Trusts Act, 1887 shall be the Official Trustees of Charitable Funds, in lieu of the persons mentioned as such in the Charitable Trusts Amendment Act, 1855.

2. The term "securities" in these regulations includes all Government or other annuities or securities, and all stocks or shares, standing in, or to be transferred into, the name of the Official Trustees of Charitable Funds, in the books of the Bank of England, or of any other Company or Corporation; and the term "funds" includes money and securities standing or to be placed to the account, or standing in or to be transferred into the name, of the said Official Trustees of Charitable Funds.

3. All moneys to be held in trust by the Official Trustees of Charitable Funds in pursuance of the Orders of the Charity Commissioners, or of Orders of Court, or of other due authority, and all dividends and interest on securities standing in the name of the said Official Trustees, shall be paid to the cash account of the said Official Trustees at the Bank of England; and all securities to be held in trust by the Official Trustees of Charitable Funds (including such securities as may be purchased by way of investment of money standing to their account) shall be transferred to or inscribed in the name of the said Official Trustees in the books of the Bank of England or other Company or Corporation in whose books such securities are registered; and the Bank of England or other Company or Corporation shall make such transfer accordingly.

4. All directions for the purchase, sale, or transfer of securities, and all orders to the Bank of England for the payment of money out of the account of the Official Trustees of Charitable Funds, shall be jointly signed by the Accountant, or in his absence the Assistant Accountant, and by one of the said Official Trustees, and be countersigned by one of the Charity Commissioners.

5. In addition to the separate ledger accounts to be kept in the Accountant's branch of the office of the Charity Commissioners for each charity in respect of which any funds are placed to the account or in the name of the Official Trustees of Charitable Funds, general ledger accounts shall be kept showing the aggregate amounts of the receipts, payments, and transfers of the several descriptions of funds distributed over the separate charity accounts, and of the balances thereof.

6. The business of the Accountant's branch of the office of the Charity Commissioners, in which the financial transactions in regard to the funds held in trust by the Official Trustees of Charitable Funds are conducted and recorded, shall be under the immediate control and responsibility of one of the said Official Trustees nominated for that purpose by the Charity Commissioners, with the concurrence of the Treasury.

7. Subject to anything contained in these regulations, the books and forms of account to be used in connexion with the funds held in trust by the Official Trustees of Charitable Funds shall be such as may from time to time be prescribed or approved by or under the authority of the Treasury.

8. . . . .

[This Regulation is printed in full at p. 38.]

9. No direction for the transfer of securities shall be given by the Official Trustees of Charitable Funds, except in pursuance of an order of the Charity Commissioners, authenticated in the manner prescribed by section 4 of the Charitable Trusts Amendment Act, 1855 (18 & 19 Vict. c. 124.).

R. E. WELBY.

Treasury, Whitehall,
27th March 1889.

(*e.*) *Exemption from Income Tax of Stock in the Public Funds held by the Official Trustees.*

[**C. T. Act, 1855.**] **28.** All Dividends arising from any Stock in the Public Funds standing in the Name of the Official Trustees of Charitable Funds, and which shall be certified by the Board to *the Governor and Company of* * the Bank of England to be exempt from the Property or Income Tax, shall be paid or carried to the Banking Account of the Official Trustees without any Deduction of such Tax; . . . *Dividends on Stock in Name of Official Trustees to be carried to Account free from Income Tax.*

[This section is printed in full at p. 42.]

(*f.*) *Annual Account to be laid before Parliament.*

[**C. T. Act, 1860.**] **18.** The Official Trustees of Charitable Funds shall lay before Parliament annually, on or before the Fourteenth Day of February, or as soon as practicable after Parliament shall be sitting, an Account of the total Amount of the Capital Stock, Shares, and Securities *Accounts to be laid before Parliament.*

[* *Repealed by the Statute Law Revision Act, 1892 (55 & 56 Vict. c. 19.).]*

E 3

transferred to them in the Year ending the Thirty-first Day of December preceding, and of the total Amount of Monies, other than Dividends or Interest, paid to them or to their Account during the same Period, and of the Investment thereof, and of the Capital Stock, Shares, and Securities sold or retransferred by them during the same Period, and of the aggregate Amount of the Capital Stock, Shares, Funds, and Securities, and the Balance of Cash, held by them on such preceding Thirty-first Day of December.

OFFICIAL TRUSTEES OF CHARITABLE FUNDS.

Regulations made by the Treasury under Section 4 of the Charitable Trusts Act, 1887 (50 & 51 Vict. c. 49).

8. The annual account to be laid before Parliament under section 18 of the Charitable Trusts Act, 1860, shall be prepared in such form as the Treasury may from time to time prescribe or approve.

[For other Treasury Regulations, see p. 36.]

(3.) *THE VESTING OR TRANSFER OF PROPERTY, OTHERWISE THAN BY ORDER OF A COURT OR JUDGE.*

(a.) *Charities generally.*

Certain administrative Powers to be exercisable by the Charity Commissioners.

[**C. T. Act, 1860.**] 2. The Board of Charity Commissioners for England and Wales, subject to the Restrictions and Rights of Appeal hereinafter provided, shall have power from Time to Time, upon the Application of any Person or Persons who, under the Forty-third Section of "The Charitable Trusts Act, 1853," might be authorized to apply to any Judge or Court for the like Purposes, to make such effectual Orders as may now be made by any Judge of the Court of Chancery sitting at Chambers, or by any County Court or *District Court of Bankruptcy,** [for the appointment or removal of Trustees of any Charity . . . . or] for or relating to the Assurance, Transfer, Payment, or vesting of any Real or Personal Estate belonging thereto, or entitling the Official Trustees of Charitable Funds, or any other Trustees, to call for a Transfer of and to transfer any Stock belonging to such Estate,† . . . .

[This section is printed in full in Appendix, No. 1, p. 75.]

By whom Applications may be made.

[**C. T. Act, 1853.**] 43. Every application to any Judge or Court under the Jurisdiction created or conferred by any of the Provisions of this Act, may be made by Her Majesty's Attorney General, or, subject to the Provisions aforesaid, by all or any One or more of the Trustees or Persons administering or claiming to administer, or interested in, the Charity which shall be the Subject of such Application, or any Two or more Inhabitants of any Parish or Place within which the Charity is administered or applicable;

[This section is printed in full in Appendix, No. 1, p. 74.]

The Powers to be exercisable over no Charities of which the gross Income shall exceed 50l. without Application of Trustees.

[**C. T. Act, 1860.**] 4. The said Board shall not make any Order, under the Jurisdiction vested in them by this Act, with respect to any Charity of which the gross annual Income, exclusively of the yearly Value of any Buildings or Land used wholly for the Purposes thereof, and not yielding any pecuniary Income, shall amount to Fifty Pounds or upwards, except upon the Application of the Trustees or Persons acting in the Administration of the Charity, or a Majority of them, to be made to the said Board in Writing under their Hands if they shall be unincorporated, or under their Common Seal if they shall be incorporated, ...

[This section is printed in full in Appendix, No. 1, p. 75.]

[* *Repealed by the Statute Law Revision Act,* 1875 (38 & 39 Vict. c. 66.).]
[† *For the jurisdiction under the Charitable Trusts Acts* (1) *of a Judge of the Chancery Division of the High Court of Justice at Chambers, see p.* 61 ; (2) *of the Chancery Court of the County Palatine of Lancaster, see p.* 64 ; *and* (3) *of the County Court, see p.* 65.]

[C. T. Act, 1869.] 5. An application to the Board of Charity Commissioners for England and Wales, for the purposes of the Charitable Trusts Acts, 1853 to 1869, when made by the trustees or persons acting in the administration of the charity, may be made in writing signed by any person authorised in that behalf by a resolution passed by a majority of those trustees or persons who are present at a meeting of their body duly constituted and vote on the question. — *Mode of application to Board.*

[C. T. Act, 1860.] 10. The Jurisdiction vested by this Act in the said Board shall be exercisable with reference to Charities vested in any Corporation Sole or Aggregate, who, either solely or jointly with any other Person or Persons, shall also be the Recipients of the Benefit thereof. — *Powers to be applicable to Charities vested in Corporations, &c.*

[C. T. Act, 1869.] 15. So much of the Charitable Trusts Acts, 1853 to 1869, as authorises and relates to orders of the Board [for the appointment or removal of trustees of a charity, or] for or relating to the vesting of any real or personal estate belonging thereto, ... shall extend to buildings registered as places of meeting for religious worship with the Registrar General of Births, Deaths, or Marriages in England, and bonâ fide used as places of meeting for religious worship: Provided that no such order shall be made except upon the application of the trustees or persons acting in the administration of the Charity, made in manner provided by section four of the Charitable Trusts Act, 1860,* or by this Act.† Save as provided by this section, such buildings shall continue exempted from the Charitable Trusts Acts, 1853 to 1869. — *Extension of part of Acts to registered places of religious worship.*

[This section is printed in full at p. 12.]

[C. T. Act, 1894.] 4. The exemption of any building registered as a place of meeting for religious worship with the Registrar-General of Births, Deaths, or Marriages in England and Wales, and bonâ fide used as a place of meeting for religious worship, contained in the sixty-second section of the Charitable Trusts Act, 1853,‡ and in the ninth section of the Places of Worship Registration Act, 1855, shall extend, and shall, without prejudice to any order of the Charity Commissioners made before the passing of this Act, be deemed to have always extended to— — *Extension of exemption in 16 & 17 Vict. c. 137, s. 62, 18 & 19 Vict. c. 81, s. 9, of places of meeting for religious worship.*

(*a*) any forecourt, yard, garden, burial-ground, vestry, or caretaker's house, in respect of situation connected with, and held upon the same trusts as, any building registered and bonâ fide used as aforesaid; and

(*b*) any Sunday-school house or other land or building which shall be certified by an order of the Charity Commissioners, made upon the application of one or more of the trustees or persons acting in the administration thereof, to be held upon the same trusts as any building registered and used as aforesaid, or upon like trusts, and to be in respect of situation so connected with or held or used in connexion with such building that it cannot conveniently be separated therefrom:

Provided always that so much of the Charitable Trusts Acts, 1853 to 1891, as by virtue of the fifteenth section of the Charitable Trusts Act, 1869, extends to buildings registered and used as aforesaid, shall also extend to the properties declared to be exempted by this Act in the same manner and subject to the same restrictions as the buildings registered and used as aforesaid. — *32 & 33 Vict. c. 110, s. 15.*

[C. T. Act, 1860.] 5. The said Board also shall not exercise the Jurisdiction hereby vested in them in any Case which, by reason of its Contentious Character, or of any special Questions of Law or of Fact which — *The Board shall not exercise Jurisdiction*

[* *See preceding page.*]   [† *Sect. 5, see supra.*]

[‡ *p. 10.*]

E 4

over Contentious Cases.

it may involve, or for other Reasons, they may consider more fit to be adjudicated on by any of the Judicial Courts.

Board to notify to Trustees of Charity their Intention of exercising Jurisdiction.

C. T. Act, 1860.] 3. The said Board, previously to making any Order under the Jurisdiction vested in them by this Act, shall notify to the Trustees or Administrators (if any) of the Charity to be affected thereby their Intention of exercising such Jurisdiction, by Notice in Writing, to be delivered to them, or sent to them by the Post, at their last known Place of Abode in Great Britain or Ireland.

Amendment of sect. 3 of 23 & 24 Vict. c. 136.

|C. T. Act, 1869.] 4. A notice under section three of the Charitable Trusts Act, 1860, need not be sent by the Board of Charity Commissioners for England and Wales to any trustee or administrator of a charity who has been party or privy to the application to the Board upon which they exercise their jurisdiction.

Indemnity to the Bank of England and others.

[C. T. Act, 1860.] 23. Every Order made under this Act under which any Stock, Shares, Securities, or Monies shall be transferred or paid to or deposited with the Trustees of any Charity, or the Official Trustees of Charitable Funds, shall afford a complete Indemnity to the Governor and Company of the Bank of England, and to all Companies and Persons by whom respectively any such Transfer, Payment, or Deposit shall be permitted or made, for permitting or making the same, and the said Governor and Company and other Companies and Persons shall be required to give effect or to conform to such Order, and it shall not be necessary for them to inquire concerning the Propriety of the same Order, or the Jurisdiction under which the same shall purport to be made.

Power to appeal against Orders of Board.

[C. T. Act, 1860.] 8. The Attorney General, or any Person authorized by him or by the said Board, in the Case of any Charity, whatever may be the yearly Income of its Endowments, and any Trustee or Person acting in the Administration of or interested in any Charity of which the gross yearly Income to be calculated in manner aforesaid* shall exceed Fifty Pounds, or any Two Inhabitants of any Parish or District in which the same shall be specially applicable, may, within Three Calendar Months next after the definitive Publication of any Order of the said Board . . . . for or relating to the Assurance, Transfer, Payment, or vesting of any Real or Personal Estate, ... present a Petition to the High Court of Chancery in a summary Way, appealing against such Order, and praying such Relief as the Case may require; . . . . and the Court, upon or before the Hearing of any such Petition of Appeal as aforesaid or at any Stage of the Proceedings, may require, if it shall think fit, from the said Board, their Reasons for making the Order appealed against, or for any Part of such Order, and may remit the same to the Board for Reconsideration, with or without any Declaration in relation thereto, or may make any substitutive or other Order in relation to the Matter of the Appeal, as it shall think just; and the Court may make any Order respecting the Costs, Charges, or Expenses incident to the Appeal, and may also, before hearing or proceeding with the same, require from any Appellant, other than the Attorney General, proper Security for such Costs, Charges, and Expenses as may be eventually payable by him; but no such Petition of Appeal shall be presented by any Person, other than the Attorney General, before the Expiration of Twenty-one Days after written Notice, under the Hand of such Appellant, of his or her Intention to present such Petition, shall have been delivered to the said Board at their Office.

[*This section is printed in full in Appendix, No. 1, p. 75.*]

Appeals under 23 & 24 Vict c. 136.

[C. T. Act, 1869.] 10. A petition to the Court of Chancery under section eight of the Charitable Trusts Act, 1860, may be presented in the case of all charities by the same persons only as in the case of a charity the gross annual income of which does not exceed fifty pounds.

[* See sect. 4 of the Charitable Trusts Act, 1860 (p. 85).]

[**C. T. Act, 1869.**] 11. A petition shall not be presented to the Court of Chancery by any person under section eight of the Charitable Trusts Act, 1860, before the expiration of twenty-one days after written notice under the hand of the appellant of his intention to present such petition has been served on the Attorney-General by delivering the same to the solicitor who acts for him in ex officio proceedings relating to charities.

Service of Attorney General by appellant under sect. 8 of 23 & 24 Vict. c. 136.

[**C. T. Act, 1860.**] 9. The Attorney General, if he shall think fit, or any Person authorized by him or by the said Board, may appear as the Respondent upon any such Appeal, and the Court may make any Order respecting the Costs, Charges, and Expenses of the Attorney General or other Defendant.

Who may be the Respondent on Appeals.

[**C. T. Act, 1869.**] 9. The Board, if they think it desirable, where the gross annual income of the charity is in their opinion sufficient to bear the expense, may, upon the application of the trustees or of any other person or persons entitled to apply to them in that behalf, ... order the costs incurred . . . . in consequence of the employment of any person to appear on behalf of the respondent upon any appeal against any . . . . order, to be provided in the same manner as if they were costs of a transaction mentioned in section thirty-six of the Charitable Trusts Act, 1855.*

Employment of persons to prepare and defend scheme.

[This section is printed in full at p. 26.]

(b.) Municipal Charities.

[**C. T. Act, 1853.**] 65. †*The legal Estate in all Lands which at the Time of the passing of the Act of the Session holden in the Fifth and Sixth Years of King William the Fourth, Chapter Seventy-six was vested in the Body Corporate of any Borough which became subject to the Provisions of the said Act, or in any One or more of the Members of such Body Corporate, in his or their corporate Capacity, solely or together with any Person or Persons elected solely by such Body Corporate, or solely by any particular Number, Class, or Description of Members of such Body Corporate, in whole or in part in trust or for the Benefit of any Charitable Uses or Trusts whatsoever, and which legal Estate shall not have been since duly conveyed or assured to and vested in the Trustees appointed by the Lord High Chancellor under the Provisions of the said Act, or such of them as shall be surviving and continuing Trustees, or otherwise lawfully conveyed, aliened, or disposed of by such Body Corporate or Member or Members thereof, shall from and immediately after the passing of this Act, and without any actual Conveyance, Assignment, or other Assurance thereof, be vested in the Trustees so appointed, or such of them as shall be surviving and continuing Trustees under such appointment as aforesaid, according to the respective Estates and Interests therein, and subject to such and the same Charges and Incumbrances and upon such and the same Trusts as the same were respectively subject to previously to such vesting; and in every Case, upon the Death, Resignation, or Removal of any of the Trustees, and upon any Appointment of any new Trustee or Trustees respectively, the legal Estate in the same Lands, and in all other Lands subject to any such Charitable Uses or Trusts which may for the Time being be vested in the Trustees or any of them, or in any Persons or the Heirs or Devisees of any Person who may have died, resigned, or been removed, shall rest in the Persons who after such Death, Resignation, or Removal, and such Appointment of such new Trustee or Trustees respectively, shall continue or be the Trustees for the Time being, without any Conveyance or Assurance whatsoever.*

Legal Estate of Lands now vested in Municipal Corporations on Charitable Trusts to be vested in Trustees. 5 & 6 W. 4. c. 76.

[**Municipal Corporations Act, 1882 (45 & 46 Vict. c. 60.).**] 133.—(1.) Where at the passing of the Municipal Corporations Act, 1835, the body corporate of a borough, or any one or more of the members thereof, in his or their corporate capacity, stood solely or together with any person or persons elected solely by that body corporate, or solely by any particular number, class,

Charitable Trusts. Administration of Charitable

[* *See p. 26.*]
[† *The whole of this section is repealed by the Municipal Corporations Act, 1882, sect. 5 (45 & 46 Vict. c. 50.); other provisions substituted by section 133 of that Act, see infra.*]

Trusts and vesting of legal estate

or description of members thereof, seised or possessed for any estate or interest of land in whole or in part in trust or for the benefit of any charitable uses or trusts, and the legal estate in that land was, at the passing of the Municipal Corporations Act, 1835, vested in the body corporate or person or persons so seised or possessed thereof, and was, by the Charitable Trusts Act, 1853, vested in the trustees appointed by the Lord Chancellor under the Municipal Corporations Act, 1835, or such of them as should be surviving and continuing trustees under that appointment, according to the respective estates and interests therein, and subject to such and the same charges and incumbrances and on such and the same trusts as the same was subject to before such vesting, then in every case on the death, resignation, or removal of any trustee, and on any appointment of a new trustee, the legal estate in that land and in all other lands subject to any such charitable uses or trusts for the time being vested in the trustees or any of them, or in any person, or the heirs or devisees of any person deceased, resigned, or removed, shall vest in the persons who, after such death, resignation, or removal, and such appointment of a new trustee, continue or are the trustees for the time being, without any conveyance or assurance.

(2.) Nothing in the section shall take away, abridge, or prejudicially affect any power, authority, or jurisdiction of the Charity Commissioners for England and Wales.

(4.) *THE DEPOSIT FOR SAFE CUSTODY AND THE ENROL-MENT OF DEEDS, WILLS, OR DOCUMENTS.*

Trustees may deposit Deeds, &c. for Security in a Repository provided by the Board.

[**C. T. Act, 1853.**] **53.** It shall be lawful for any Trustees or other Persons having the Custody of any Deeds or Muniments of or relating to such Charity to deposit the same for Security in a Repository which may be provided by the said Board, subject to any Regulations to be made by the said Board under this Act.

Power to require the Transmission of Documents belonging to Charities.

[**C. T. Act, 1860.**] **19.** The Board may require any Person having the Custody or Control of any Deed or Document in which any Charity or Charities shall be solely interested to transmit the same to the Office of the said Commissioners for Examination ; and where such Deed or Document shall not be held by any Person entitled as a Trustee or otherwise to the Custody thereof, the Board may either retain the same, for the Security thereof, in the Repository provided by them under the Sixty-third* Section of "The Charitable Trusts Act, 1853," or, as they may think most advantageous to the Charity, may thereupon, or at any Time thereafter, return or issue the same to the Trustees or Persons acting in the Administration of the Charity, for the Purposes thereof.

Deeds, &c. relating to Charities may be enrolled at the Office, and Copies to be Evidence.

[**C. T. Act, 1855.**] **42.** Any Deed, Will, or Document relating to any Charity may be enrolled by the Board in Books to be provided and kept by them for that Purpose at their Office, and a Copy of any such Deed, Will, or Document made from such Books, and certified under the Hand of the Secretary† or One of the Commissioners, shall be received as Evidence of the Contents of the same Deed, Will, or Document.

(5.) *THE EXEMPTION FROM INCOME TAX OF DIVIDENDS UPON STOCK IN THE PUBLIC FUNDS.*

Dividends on Stock in Name of Official Fund Trustees to be carried to Account free from Income Tax.

[**C. T. Act, 1855.**] **28.** All Dividends arising from any Stock in the Public Funds standing in the Name of the Official Trustees of Charitable Funds, and which shall be certified by the Board to *the Governor and Company of*‡ the Bank of England to be exempt from the Property or Income Tax, shall be paid or carried to the Banking Account of the Official Trustees without any Deduction of such Tax ; and all Dividends arising from any Stock in the Public Funds standing in any other Names or Name, and which the Board shall certify to *the Governor and Company of*‡ the Bank of England to be subject only to Charitable Trusts, and to be exempt from such Tax, shall be paid without any Deduction thereof.

[* *Should be " Fifty-third."*]

[† *or any officer of the Board duly authorised to act on behalf of the Secretary. See Charitable Trusts Act, 1887, sect. 3. (p. 16).*]

[‡ *Repealed by the Statute Law Revision Act, 1892 (55 & 56 Vict. c. 19.).*]

(6.) *THE TAXATION OF BILLS OF COSTS.*

[**C. T. Act, 1855.**] **40.** The Board may order the Bill of Costs or Charges claimed by any Attorney or Solicitor on account of Business conducted or transacted by him on behalf of any Charity, or the Trustees thereof, to be examined and taxed by the Taxing Masters of the Court of Chancery, or by the proper Taxing Officers of any of the Superior Courts at Westminster, who shall proceed to examine and tax the same Bill accordingly; and if the same shall be reduced upon such Taxation by the Amount of One Sixth Part or more of the Amount thereof, the Costs of the Taxation shall be paid by such Attorney or Solicitor, but otherwise out of the Funds of the Charity by the Trustees thereof; and the Board may, after being satisfied as to any Bill that it contains exorbitant Charges order any such Bill to be so taxed, notwithstanding that the same may have been paid by the Trustees of the Charity at any Period not more than Six Calendar Months previously to such Order; and any Amount taxed off any such paid Bill shall be a Debt due from the Attorney or Solicitor to the Trustees of the Charity, and shall be forthwith paid by him to such Trustees accordingly.

Power to refer Bills of Costs in Charity Matters to Taxation.

VIII.—Provisions conferring on the Charity Commissioners Powers for the Appointment and Removal of Trustees of Charities.

(*a.*) *AS INCIDENTAL TO ORDERS FOR THE APPORTIONMENT OF CHARITIES.*

[**C. T. Act, 1855.**] **10.** Where any Parish or Ecclesiastical District entitled to the Benefit of a Charity has or shall have been divided into separate Parishes or Ecclesiastical Districts, and no Apportionment of Charities originally applicable to the Parish or District so divided shall have been made by Parliament or other competent Authority, the Board, in respect of all Charities the gross annual Income whereof does not for the Time being exceed Thirty Pounds, may apportion the Benefit of the Charity between each new Parish or District, or any Portion thereof taken from the Parish or District originally entitled to the whole Benefit, and the Remainder of such last-mentioned Parish or District, in such Manner and such Proportions as, upon a Consideration of the Purposes of the Charity, the Population of each Parish or District, and other Circumstances, they may think fit, and may also apportion the principal Endowments between such Parishes or Districts, if it be thought fit, and may appoint separate Trustees of any Part of the Endowments.

Power to apportion Parochial Charities after Division of Parishes.

[**C. T. Act, 1855.**] **11.** The Certificate of the Board, that according to their Judgment the gross yearly Income of the Charity does not for the Time being exceed Thirty Pounds, shall be sufficient Evidence of the Amount of such annual Income for the Purpose of determining the Jurisdiction under the foregoing Provision.

Evidence as to annual Income of any Charity not exceeding 30l.

[**C. T. Act, 1855.**] **13.** No Order for apportioning the Benefits of any Charity shall be made by the Board until after such public Notices shall have been given of the Proposal to make the same as the Board may consider expedient for insuring Publicity in each Parish or District in which the Charity is or ought to be applied, or among all Persons interested therein, nor until after the Expiration of One Month from the Publication of such Notice; and every such Notice shall contain (so far as conveniently may

Notices to be given of certain Orders of the Board.

be) sufficient Particulars of the proposed Order to show the Objects thereof, and shall prescribe a Time within which any Objections thereto may be stated or transmitted to the Board.

[C. T. Act, 1855.] 14. All Objections which may be made to any proposed Order shall be considered by the Board, who may suspend the making thereof for further Inquiry, or may modify the same, as may be found expedient ; and a Copy of every such Order when made shall, in the Case of any local Charity, be deposited for the Space of One Month in some convenient Place within the Parish or One of the Parishes or the District in which the Charity is applicable, and also be open to Inspection at the Office of the Commissioners, and such Publicity shall be given thereto among all Persons interested in the Charity as the Board shall consider expedient ; or if the Charity be not local, then a Copy of such Order shall be open to Inspection at the Office of the Commissioners, and public Notice thereof shall be given in such Manner as to the Board shall seem fit, and in Cases where there is a special Visitor, Notice shall be given to him.

Proceedings upon the Receipt of Objections or Suggestions.

(b.) *GENERALLY.*

[C. T. Act, 1860.] 2. The Board of Charity Commissioners for England and Wales, subject to the Restrictions and Rights of Appeal herein-after provided, shall have Power from Time to Time, upon the Application of any Person or Persons who, under the Forty-third Section of " The Charitable Trusts Act, 1853," might be authorized to apply to any Judge or Court for the like Purposes, to make such effectual Orders as may now be made by any Judge of the Court of Chancery sitting at Chambers, or by any County Court *or District Court of Bankruptcy,** for the Appointment or Removal of Trustees of any Charity, ...

Certain administrative Powers to be exercisable by the Charity Commissioners.

[*This section is printed in full in Appendix, No.* 1, *p.* 75.]

[C. T. Act, 1862.] Whereas by the Acts relating to the Charity Commissioners for England and Wales, Authority has been given to the Commissioners to make Orders for various Purposes in Charity Cases upon summary Application, and particularly in relation to the Appointment and Removal of Trustees, .   .   : And whereas in various Private Acts of Parliament and Decrees and Orders of the High Court of Chancery relating to Charities such Powers and Authorities are often given or reserved, with Directions that the same shall be exercised by the said Court, or with its Sanction or Approbation, and Doubts are entertained whether in such Cases the Authority given to the Charity Commissioners can be validly exercised : Be it therefore enacted and declared *by the Queen's most Excellent Majesty, by and with the advice and consent of the Lords Spiritual and Temporal, and Commons, in this present Parliament assembled, and by the authority of the same,†* as follows :

1. No Provision contained in any such Act of Parliament or Decree or Order as aforesaid for the Appointment or Removal of Trustees of any Charity, ... by or under the Order or with the Approval of the Court of Chancery, shall (in the Absence of any express Direction to the contrary, to be contained in any future Act of Parliament, Order, or Decree,) exclude or impair any Jurisdiction or Authority which might otherwise be properly exercised for the like Purposes by the Charity Commissioners for England and Wales.

No provision in any Act of Parliament, or Decree relating to any Charity under any Order of the Court of Chancery, to exclude any Jurisdiction which might otherwise be exercised by the Charity Commissioners.

[*This section and the preamble are printed in full in Appendix, No.* 1, *p.* 76.]

[C. T. Act, 1853.] 43. Every Application to any Judge or Court under the Jurisdiction created or conferred by any of the Provisions of this Act, may be made by Her Majesty's Attorney General, or, subject to the Provisions aforesaid, by all or any One or more of the Trustees or Persons administering or claiming to administer, or interested in, the Charity which

By whom Applications may be made.

[* *Repealed by the Statute Law Revision Act,* 1875 (38 & 39 Vict. c. 66.).]
[† *Repealed by the Statute Law Revision Act,* 1893 (56 Vict. c. 14.).]

shall be the Subject of such Application, or any Two or more Inhabitants of any Parish or Place within which the Charity is administered or applicable ; . . . .

[This section is printed in full in Appendix, No. 1, p. 74.]

[C. T. Act, 1860.] 4. The said Board shall not make any Order, under the Jurisdiction vested in them by this Act, with respect to any Charity of which the gross annual Income, exclusively of the yearly Value of any Buildings or Land used wholly for the Purposes thereof, and not yielding any pecuniary Income, shall amount to Fifty Pounds or upwards, except upon the application of the Trustees or Persons acting in the Administration of the Charity, or a Majority of them to be made to the said Board in Writing under their Hands if they shall be unincorporated, or under their Common Seal if they shall be incorporated, ...

The Powers to be exercisable over no Charities of which the gross Income shall exceed 50l. without Application of Trustees.

[This section is printed in full in Appendix, No. 1, p. 75.]

[C. T. Act, 1869.] 5. An application to the Board of Charity Commissioners for England and Wales, for the purposes of the Charitable Trusts Acts, 1853 to 1869, when made by the trustees or persons acting in the administration of the Charity, may be made in writing signed by any person authorised in that behalf by resolution passed by a majority of those Trustees or persons who are present at a meeting of their body duly constituted and vote on the question.

Mode of application to Board.

[C. T. Act, 1860.] 10. The Jurisdiction vested by this Act in the said Board shall be exercisable with reference to Charities vested in any Corporation Sole or Aggregate, who, either solely or jointly with any other Person or Persons, shall also be the Recipients of the Benefit thereof.

Powers to be applicable to Charities vested in Corporations, &c.

[C. T. Act, 1869.] 15. So much of the Charitable Trusts Acts, 1853 to 1869, as authorises and relates to orders of the Board for the appointment or removal of trustees of a charity, ... shall extend to buildings registered as places of meeting for religious worship with the Registrar General of Births, Deaths, or Marriages in England, and bonâ fide used as places of meeting of religious worship : Provided that no such order shall be made except upon the application of the trustees or persons acting in the administration of the charity, made in manner provided by section four of the Charitable Trusts Act, 1860,* or by this Act.† Save as provided by this section, such buildings shall continue exempted from the Charitable Trusts Acts, 1853 to 1869.

Extension of part of Acts to registered places of religious worship.

[This section is printed in full at p. 12.]

[C. T. Act, 1894.] 4. The exemption of any building registered as a place of meeting for religious worship with the Registrar-General of Births, Deaths, or Marriages in England and Wales, and bonâ fide used as a place of meeting for religious worship, contained in the sixty-second section of the Charitable Trusts Act, 1853, and in the ninth section of the Places of Worship Registration Act, 1855, shall extend, and shall, without prejudice to any order of the Charity Commissioners made before the passing of this Act, be deemed to have always extended to—

Extension of exemption in 16 & 17 Vict. c. 137. s. 62. 18 & 19 Vict. c. 81. s. 9, of places of meeting for religious worship.

(*a*) any forecourt, yard, garden, burial-ground, vestry, or caretaker's house, in respect of situation connected with, and held upon the same trusts as, any building registered and bonâ fide used as aforesaid ; and

(*b*) any Sunday-school house or other land or building which shall be certified by an order of the Charity Commissioners, made upon the application of one or more of the trustees or persons acting in the administration thereof, to be held upon the same trusts as any building registered and used as aforesaid, or upon like trusts, and to be in respect of situation so connected with or held or used in

[* *See supra.*]   †† *Sect. 5, see supra.*]

F 3

connexion with such building that it cannot conveniently be separated therefrom:

Provided always that so much of the Charitable Trusts Acts, 1853 to 1891, as by virtue of the fifteenth section of the Charitable Trusts Act, 1869, extends to buildings registered and used as aforesaid, shall also extend to the properties declared to be exempted by this Act in the same manner and subject to the same restrictions as the buildings registered and used as aforesaid.

[C. T. Act, 1853.] 46. Nothing herein contained shall diminish or detract from any Right or Privilege which by any Rule or Practice of the Court of Chancery, or by the Construction of Law, now subsists for the Preference or the exclusive or special Benefit of the Church of England, or the Members of the same Church, [in settling any Scheme for the Regulation of any Charity, or] in the Appointment or Removal of Trustees, [or generally in the Application or Management of any Charity].

[C. T. Act, 1860.] 4. . . . . And the Board shall not make any Order removing any Trustee on the Ground only of his Religious Belief.

[*This section is printed in full in Appendix, No. 1, p. 75.*]

[C. T. Act, 1860.] 5. The said Board also shall not exercise the Jurisdiction hereby vested in them in any Case which, by reason of its Contentious Character, or of any special Questions of Law or of Fact which it may involve, or for other Reasons, they may consider more fit to be adjudicated on by any of the Judicial Courts.

[C. T. Act, 1860.] 3. The said Board, previously to making any Order under the Jurisdiction vested in them by this Act, shall notify to the Trustees or Administrators (if any) of the Charity to be effected thereby their Intention of exercising such Jurisdiction, by Notice in Writing, to be delivered to them, or sent to them by the Post at their last known Place of Abode in Great Britain or Ireland.

[C. T. Act, 1869.] 4. A notice under section three of the Charitable Trusts Act, 1860, need not be sent by the Board of Charity Commissioners for England and Wales to any trustee or administrator of a charity who has been party or privy to the application to the Board upon which they exercise their jurisdiction.

[C. T. Act, 1860.] 6. No Order appointing or removing a Trustee, ... shall be made by the said Board before the Expiration of One Calendar Month after public Notice of the Proposal to make such Order shall have been given, as they may consider most expedient and effectual for ensuring the Publicity thereof, in each Parish or District in which the Charity, if of a local Character, shall be applicable, or among all Persons interested therein; and no Order removing a Trustee . . . . of a Charity who shall have any known Place of Residence in Great Britain or Ireland, and who shall not be consenting to be discharged, shall be made before the Expiration of One Calendar Month after Notice of the Proposal to make such Order shall have also been delivered to him or her, or sent by the Post or otherwise to such his or her Place of Residence, and until after sufficient Hearing of the Matter before the said Board, or some Member thereof, or One of their *Inspectors** ; and every Notice hereby required shall contain (so far as conveniently may be) sufficient Particulars of the Objects of the proposed Order, and shall prescribe a reasonable Time within which any Objections thereto or Suggestions thereon may be made or transmitted to the Board ; and the said Board shall receive and consider all such Objections and Suggestions, and may withhold, suspend, or modify their

[* *Note* "*Assistant Commissioners.*" *See Charitable Trusts Act, 1887, sect.* 2, *sub-sect.* 3 (*p.* 13).]

proposed Order, as they shall thereupon, or in the Result of further Inquiry, or otherwise, think expedient.

[This section is printed in full in Appendix, No. 1, p. 75.]

[C. T. Act, 1869.] 7. Nothing in the Charitable Trusts Acts, 1853 to 1869, shall be deemed to require or to have required the Board, upon modifying a proposed order in manner provided by section six of the Charitable Trusts Act, 1860, after the publication thereof, to give public notice of such modified order in the manner provided by that section with respect to the order originally proposed, unless they think further notice desirable.

Notice of order. 23 & 24 Vict. c. 136. s. 6.

[C. T. Act, 1860.] 7. A Copy of every such Order when made shall, in the Case of any local Charity, be deposited for the Space of One Calendar Month in some convenient Place within the Parish or One of the Parishes or in the District in which the Charity shall be applicable, and shall be open to public Inspection there at all reasonable Hours during the same Period ; and a Copy also of every such Order relating to any Charity, whether local or general, shall be kept open to public Inspection at all reasonable Hours, at the Office of the Commissioners, during a like period of One Calendar Month ; and in each Case effectual Publicity shall be given to the making of the Order by such Means as the Board shall consider most expedient for that Purpose.

Publication of definitive Orders.

[C. T. Act, 1860.] 8. The Attorney General, or any Person authorized by him or by the said Board, in the Case of any Charity, whatever may be the yearly income of its Endowments, and any Trustee or Person acting in the Administration of or interested in any Charity of which the gross yearly Income to be calculated in manner aforesaid* shall exceed Fifty Pounds, or any Two Inhabitants of any Parish or District in which the same shall be specially applicable, may, within Three Calendar Months next after the definitive Publication of any Order of the said Board appointing or removing a Trustee or Trustees, ... present a Petition to the High Court of Chancery in a summary Way, appealing against such Order, and praying such Relief as the Case may require ; . . . . . ; and the Court, upon or before the Hearing of any such Petition of Appeal as aforesaid or at any Stage of the Proceedings, may require, if it shall think fit, from the said Board, their Reasons for making the Order appealed against, or for any Part of such Order, and may remit the same to the Board for Reconsideration, with or without any Declaration in relation thereto, or may make any substitutive or other Order in relation to the Matter of the Appeal, as it shall think just ; and the Court may make any Order respecting the Costs, Charges, or Expenses incident to the Appeal, and may also, before hearing or proceeding with the same, require from any Appellant, other than the Attorney General, proper security for such Costs, Charges, and Expenses as may be eventually payable by him ; but no such Petition of Appeal shall be presented by any Person, other than the Attorney General, before the Expiration of Twenty-one Days after written Notice, under the Hand of such Appellant, of his or her Intention to present such Petition, shall have been delivered to the said Board at their Office.

Power to appeal against Orders of Board.

[This section is printed in full in Appendix, No. 1, p. 75.]

[C. T. Act, 1869.] 10. A petition to the Court of Chancery under section eight of the Charitable Trusts Act, 1860, may be presented in the case of all charities by the same persons only as in the case of a charity the gross annual income of which does not exceed fifty pounds.

Appeals under 23 & 24 V c. 136

[C. T. Act, 1869.] 11. A petition shall not be presented to the Court of Chancery by any person under section eight of the Charitable Trusts Act, 1860, before the expiration of twenty-one days after written notice under the hand of the appellant of his intention to present such petition has been served

Service of Attorney General by appellant under

[* *See section 1 of the Charitable Trusts Act, 1860 (p. 45).*]

F 4

sect. 8 of
23 & 24 Vict.
c. 136.

on the Attorney-General by delivering the same to the solicitor who acts for him in ex-officio proceedings relating to charities.

Who may be
the Respon-
dent on
Appeals.

[**C. T. Act, 1860.**]   **9.** The Attorney General, if he shall think fit, or any Person authorized by him or by the said Board, may appear as the Respondent upon any such Appeal, and the Court may make any Order respecting the Costs, Charges, and Expenses of the Attorney General or other Defendant.

Employment
of persons to
prepare and
defend
scheme.

[**C. T. Act, 1869.**]   **9.** The Board, if they think it desirable, where the gross annual income of a charity is in their opinion sufficient to bear the expense, may, upon the application of the trustees or of any other person or persons entitled to apply to them in that behalf, ... order the costs incurred . . . . in consequence of the employment of any person to appear on behalf of the respondent upon any appeal against any order, to be provided in the same manner as if they were costs of a transaction mentioned in section thirty-six of the Charitable Trusts Acts, 1855.*

[*This section is printed in full at p. 26.*]

IX.—Provisions conferring on the Charity Commissioners Powers for, or in Relation to, the removal of School Masters, or other Officers, or recipients of Charities.

Commis-
sioners to
authorize
Trustees to
remove
Officers.

[**C. T. Act, 1853.**]   **22.** It shall be lawful for the Board upon proof to their Satisfaction that any Schoolmaster or Schoolmistress or other Officer of any Charity has been negligent in performing his or her Duties, or that he or she is unfit or incompetent to discharge them properly, either from immoral Conduct, Age, or any other Cause whatsoever, to empower the Trustees of such Charity to remove such School Master or Mistress or other Officer, and to charge the Salary of his or her Successors, or any other Portion of the Revenues of the Charity, with such Retiring Pension or Allowance, if any, in favour of the Person so removed, and generally to impose such Conditions as to the said Board shall appear proper: Provided always, that where there shall be any special Visitor of the Charity, the Consent of such Visitor, in Writing under his Hand, shall be necessary in order to such removal.

Masters and
Mistresses of
Endowed
Schools to be
removable.

[**C. T. Act, 1860.**]   **14.** Every School Master and Mistress appointed after the Date of this Act shall be removable from his or her Office, after reasonable Notice by the Trustees or Persons acting in the Administration of the Charity, as they shall think expedient in the Interests thereof, so nevertheless that the Removal by virtue only of this Provision of a Master or Mistress who would be otherwise irremovable from his or her Office shall be determined on by all or a Majority of such Trustees or Administrators assembled at a Meeting convened by due Notice, delivered or sent by the Post to all such Trustees or Administrators who shall have any known Place of Residence in Great Britain or Ireland, by the Space of not less than Twenty-eight Days previously, for the special Purpose of considering and determining on the Question of such Removal, and of which intended Meeting a Notice shall also be delivered or sent in like Manner to the Master or Mistress by the same previous Space, and so also that the Resolution of the Meeting for the Removal of any such last-mentioned Master or Mistress shall be forthwith certified under the Hands of the Trustees or Persons acting as aforesaid who shall have concurred therein, or under the Hand of the Chairman of the Meeting, and shall within Seven Days next thereafter be transmitted to the said Board for their Approval, and the

[* For this section, see p. 29.]

same shall not take effect unless or until the same shall have been approved by the said Board, who may also, if they so think fit, fix the Time or any reasonable Conditions at or under which the same shall come into operation; if also there shall be any Special Visitor of the Charity who shall be resident in Great Britain or Ireland, and free from Incapacity, no Removal of any such last-mentioned Master or Mistress shall be made under the Authority only of the preceding Provision without the written Consent of such Visitor: Provided always, that this Section shall not apply to any endowed Grammar School.

[C. T. Act, 1860.] 2. The Board of Charity Commissioners for England and Wales, subject to the Restrictions and Rights of Appeal hereinafter provided, shall have power from Time to Time, upon the Application of any Person or Persons who, under the Forty-third Section of " The Charitable Trusts Act, 1853," might be authorized to apply to any Judge or Court for the like purposes, to make such effectual Orders as may now be made by any Judge of the Court of Chancery sitting at Chambers, or by any County Court *or District Court of Bankruptcy* * [for the Appointment or Removal of Trustees of any Charity, or] for the Removal of any School Master or Mistress or other Officer thereof.† . . . .

Certain administrative Powers to be exercisable by the Charity Commissioners.

[This section is printed in full in Appendix, No. 1, p. 75.]

[C. T. Act, 1853.] 43. Every Application to any Judge or Court under the Jurisdiction created or conferred by any of the Provisions of this Act, may be made by Her Majesty's Attorney General, or, subject to the Provisions aforesaid, by all or any One or more of the Trustees or Persons administering or claiming to administer, or interested in, the Charity which shall be the Subject of such Application, or any Two or more Inhabitants of any Parish or Place within which the Charity is administered or applicable; . . . . .

By whom Applications may be made.

[This section is printed in full in Appendix, No. 1, p. 74.]

[C. T. Act, 1860.] 4. The said Board shall not make any Order, under the Jurisdiction vested in them by this Act, with respect to any Charity of which the gross annual Income, exclusively of the yearly Value of any Buildings or Land used wholly for the Purposes thereof, and not yielding any pecuniary Income, shall amount to Fifty Pounds or upwards, except upon the Application of the Trustees or Persons acting in the Administration of the Charity, or a majority of them, to be made to the said Board in Writing under their Hands if they shall be unincorporated, or under their Common Seal if they shall be incorporated, ...

The Powers to be exercisable over no Charities of which the gross Income shall exceed 50l. without Application of Trustees.

[This section is printed in full in Appendix, No. 1, p. 75.]

[C. T. Act, 1869.] 5. An application to the Board of Charity Commissioners for England and Wales, for the purposes of the Charitable Trusts Acts, 1853 to 1869, when made by the trustees or persons acting in the administration of the charity, may be made in writing signed by any person authorised in that behalf by a resolution passed by a majority of those trustees or persons who are present at a meeting of their body duly constituted and vote on the question.

Mode of application to Board.

[C. T. Act, 1860.] 10. The Jurisdiction vested by this Act in the said Board, shall be exercisable with reference to Charities vested in any Corporation Sole or Aggregate, who, either solely or jointly with any other Person or Persons, shall also be the Recipients of the Benefit thereof.

Powers to be applicable to Charities vested in Corporations, &c.

[* *Repealed by the Statute Law Revision Act, 1875 (38 & 39 Vict. c. 66).*]
[† *For the jurisdiction under the Charitable Trusts Acts (1) of a Judge of the Chancery Division of the High Court of Justice at Chambers, see p. 61: (2) of the Chancery Court of the County Palatine of Lancaster, see p. 64; and (3) of the County Courts, see p. 65.*]

The Board shall not exercise Jurisdiction over Contentious Cases.

[**C. T. Act, 1860.**] 5. The said Board shall not exercise the Jurisdiction hereby vested in them in any Case which by reason of its Contentious Character, or of any special Questions of Law or of Fact which it may involve, or for other Reasons, they may consider more fit to be adjudicated on by any of the Judicial Courts.

Board to notify to Trustees of Charity their Intention of exercising Jurisdiction.

[**C. T. Act, 1860.**] 3. The said Board, previously to making any Order under the Jurisdiction vested in them by this Act, shall notify to the Trustees or Administrators (if any) of the Charity to be effected thereby their Intention of exercising such Jurisdiction, by Notice in Writing, to be delivered to them, or sent to them by the Post at their last known Place of Abode in Great Britain or Ireland.

Amendment of sect. 3 of 23 & 24 Vict. c. 136.

[**C. T. Act, 1869.**] 4. A notice under section three of the Charitable Trusts Act, 1860, need not be sent by the Board of Charity Commissioners for England and Wales to any trustee or administrator of a charity who has been party or privy to the application to the Board upon which they exercise their jurisdiction.

Notices to be given of certain Orders, and Objections or Suggestions to be received.

[**C. T. Act, 1860.**] 6. . . . . and no Order removing a . . . . School Master or Mistress or other Officer of a Charity who shall have any known Place of Residence in Great Britain or Ireland, and who shall not be consenting to be discharged, shall be made before the Expiration of One Calendar Month after Notice of the Proposal to make such Order shall have also been delivered to him or her, or sent by the Post or otherwise to such his or her Place of Residence, and until after sufficient Hearing of the Matter before the said Board, or some Member thereof, or One of their *Inspectors**; and every Notice hereby required shall contain (so far as conveniently may be) sufficient Particulars of the Objects of the proposed Order, and shall prescribe a reasonable Time within which any Objections thereto or Suggestions thereon may be made or transmitted to the Board; and the said Board shall receive and consider all such Objections and Suggestions, and may withhold, suspend, or modify their proposed Order, as they shall thereupon, or in the Result of further Inquiry, or otherwise, think expedient.

[*This section is printed in full in Appendix, No. 1, p. 75.*]

Power to appeal against Orders of Board.

[**C. T. Act, 1860.**] 8. . . . . .; and any Schoolmaster or Schoolmistress or other Officer removed by Order of the Board, without the Concurrence of the Trustees or Persons acting in the Administration of the Charity, or a Majority of them, and without the Approval of a Special Visitor, if any, of the Charity, may, within Two Calendar Months (next after his or her Removal), appeal in like Manner† against the Order of Removal; and the Court, upon or before the Hearing of any such Petition of Appeal as aforesaid or at any Stage of the Proceedings, may require, if it shall think fit, from the said Board, their Reasons for making the Order appealed against, or for any Part of such Order, and may remit the same to the Board for Reconsideration, with or without any Declaration in relation thereto, or may make any substitutive or other Order in relation to the Matter of the Appeal, as it shall think just; and the Court may make any Order respecting the Costs, Charges, or Expenses incident to the Appeal, and may also, before hearing or proceeding with the same, require from any Appellant, other than the Attorney General, proper Security for such Costs, Charges, and Expenses as may be eventually payable by him; but no such Petition or Appeal shall be presented by any Person, other than the Attorney General, before the Expiration of Twenty-one Days after written Notice, under the Hand of such Appellant, of his or her Intention to present such Petition, shall have been delivered to the said Board at their Office.

[*This section is printed in full in Appendix, No. 1, p. 75.*]

[* *Now "Assistant Commissioners." See the Charitable Trusts Act, 1887, sect. 2, sub-sect. 3 (p. 13).*]

[† *The mode of appeal prescribed by the preceding portion of this section is by petition to the High Court of Chancery; see Appendix, No. 1, p. 75, where the section is printed in full.*]

[C. T. Act, 1869.] 11. A petition shall not be presented to the Court of Chancery by any person under section eight of the Charitable Trusts Act, 1860, before the expiration of twenty-one days after written notice under the hand of the appellant of his intention to present such petition has been served on the Attorney General by delivering the same to the solicitor who acts for him in ex officio proceedings relating to charities.

Service of Attorney General by appellant under sect. 8 of 23 & 24 Vict. c. 136.

[C. T. Act, 1860.] 9. The Attorney General, if he shall think fit, or any Person authorized by him or by the said Board, may appear as the Respondent upon any such Appeal, and the Court may make any Order respecting the Costs, Charges, and Expenses of the Attorney General or other Defendant.

Who may be the Respondent on Appeals.

[C. T. Act, 1869.] 9. The Board, if they think it desirable, where the gross annual income of a charity is in their opinion sufficient to bear the expense, may, upon the application of the trustees or of any other person or persons entitled to apply to them in that behalf, ... order the costs incurred . . . . in consequence of the employment of any person to appear on behalf of the respondent upon any appeal against any order, to be provided in the same manner as if they were costs of a transaction mentioned in section thirty-six of the Charitable Trusts Act, 1855.*

Employment of persons to prepare and defend scheme.

[This section is printed in full at p. 26.]

[C. T. Act, 1860.] 13. Where any School Master or Mistress or other Officer, or any Recipient of the Benefit of a Charity, being in possession by virtue of his or her Office, or as such Recipient, of any House, Buildings, Land, or Property of the Charity, shall have been removed from or shall cease to hold such his or her Office, or his or her Place as such Recipient, but he or she, or any Person claiming under him or her, shall refuse or neglect to relinquish the Possession of such House, Buildings, Land, or Property within One Calendar Month next thereafter, to his or her Successor, or to the Trustees or Persons acting in the Administration of the Charity, or as they shall direct, it shall be lawful for any Two or more Justices of the Peace acting for the District, Division, or Place in which such House, Buildings, Land, or Property shall be situate, in Petty Sessions assembled, and they are hereby required, on the Complaint of the said Trustees or Administrators, and on the Production of an Order of the said Board certifying such School Master or Mistress or other Officer or Recipient to have been duly removed from or to have ceased to hold his or her Office or Place, (which Order under the Seal of the said Commissioners shall be conclusive Evidence of the Facts thereby certified, and of the Jurisdiction of the said Commissioners to make such Order for all the Purposes of this Enactment, and shall afford a complete Indemnity to all Persons acting thereunder,) to issue a Warrant under the Hands and Seals of such Justices to any Constables or Peace Officers of the same District, Division, or Place, commanding them, within a Period to be thereby appointed, not being less than Ten or more than Twenty-one clear Days thereafter, to enter into the Premises, and deliver Possession thereof to the said Trustees or Administrators, or their Nominee or Agent, and to remove therefrom such former School Master or Mistress, or other Officer or Recipient, and all Persons claiming in his or her Right, as fully and effectually, and subject to the same Provisions, as nearly as the Case will permit, as Justices of the Peace are empowered to give Possession of any Properties to the Landlord or his Agent upon the Determination of the Tenancy thereof, under an Act passed in the First and Second Years of the Reign of Her Majesty, Chapter Seventy-four, for facilitating the Recovery of Possession of Tenements after the Determination of the Tenancy.

Power for Magistrates to give Possession of School Buildings and Property held over by Officers or Recipients of Charities.

[* For this section, see p. 29.]

X.—Provisions for the Administration of Charities, and for the Application of the Endowments and Income thereof by means of—

    (*a.*) *SCHEMES ESTABLISHED BY THE ACTION OF PARLIAMENT.*

    (*b.*) *SCHEMES ESTABLISHED BY THE CHARITY COMMISSIONERS.*

    (*c.*) *ORDERS MADE BY THE CHARITY COMMISSIONERS FOR THE APPORTIONMENT OF CHARITIES.*

(*a.*) SCHEMES ESTABLISHED BY THE ACTION OF PARLIAMENT.

Power to Board to frame Schemes for the Appropriation of Charitable Property to varied Trusts.

[**C. T. Act, 1853.**] **54.** Where upon the Application of any Trustees or other Persons concerned in the Management or Administration of any Charity, or interested in the Benefits thereof (and after such Examination or Inquiry as the Board may think necessary in relation thereto,) or upon any Report of an *Inspector*,* or Information otherwise obtained by the said Board under this Act, with relation to any Charity, it shall appear to the said Board to be desirable to have a new Scheme for the Application or Management of the Charity, and such new Scheme as contemplated or considered desirable by the Board cannot be, or it shall in the Opinion of the Board be doubtful whether it can be carried into complete effect by the Court of Chancery, or by any *District or* †County Court under the Jurisdiction created by this Act, or otherwise than by the Authority of Parliament, it shall be lawful for the said Board in every such Case provisionally to approve and certify such new Scheme in the Manner and subject to the Regulations herein-after mentioned.

Notice to be given before Approval of Schemes, and Objections may be submitted for the Consideration of the Board.

[**C. T. Act, 1853.**] **55.** One Month at least before any such new Scheme shall be so provisionally approved, Notice thereof shall be given in such Manner as the Board may in each Case consider proper or expedient for ensuring due Publicity, and every such Notice shall contain such Particulars of the proposed Scheme as the said Board think fit, and as shall be deemed by the said Board sufficient to show the Nature of such Scheme, and where the Nature thereof cannot conveniently be shown in the said Notice, such Notice shall refer to some convenient Place within the Parish or District, and to *the Office in London of the Registrar of County Courts Judgments*, where a Copy of the proposed Scheme shall be deposited and may be inspected, and every such Notice shall require any Objections to such Scheme to be stated or transmitted to the said Board or their Secretary within One Month from the Time when the Notice shall have been given.

Construction of Sects. 55. and 59. of 16 & 17 Vict. c. 137.

[**C. T. Act, 1855.**] **43.** The Fifty-fifth . . . . Section(s) of the principal Act shall be construed and operate as if the Words " The Office of the Board " had been inserted therein in the Place of the Words " the Office in London of the Registrar of County Courts Judgments."

[*This section is printed in full at p. 72.*]

Board may alter or modify or approve of Schemes.

[**C. T. Act, 1853.**] **56.** If after such Notice as aforesaid any Objections or Suggestions shall be made, the Board shall consider the same, and may thereupon, if to them it shall seem fit, alter or modify the Scheme according to any such Objections or Suggestions; and after all such Objections and Suggestions, if any, have been disposed of, or if no such Objections or Suggestions shall have been made, the Board, in case they shall not think fit to refer such Scheme to an *Inspector** under the Provision next herein-after contained, may proceed to approve such Scheme, and to certify the same in manner herein-after mentioned.

[* *Now " Assistant Commissioner," or " Assistant Commissioners," as context may require. See the Charitable Trusts Act, 1887, sect. 2, subsect. 3 (p. 131.)*]

[† *Repealed by the Statute Law Revision Act, 1892 (55 & 56 Vict. c. 19).*]

[**C. T. Act, 1853.**] **57.** Upon the Requisition of any Person interested in the Charity in question (in case the said Board after due Consideration shall be of Opinion that there are sufficient Grounds for complying with such Requisition), or in any other Case, if the said Board shall consider it desirable, the Matter of any Scheme in question may be referred by the said Board to One of their *Inspectors*,* and such *Inspector** shall thereupon proceed to make a local Inquiry and Examination into the Matter of the Scheme in question, and for the Purposes of such Inquiry, such *Inspector** may hold a Sitting or Sittings in some convenient Place in the Parish or One of the Parishes or the District to or in which respectively the Charity in question is wholly or partially situated or is administered, and may take and receive any Evidence and Information, and hear and inquire into any Objections or Questions relating to the Scheme or Charity in question, and may from Time to Time adjourn any such Sitting, and public Notice shall be given by such *Inspector** of every such Sitting (except an adjourned Sitting) Fourteen Days at the least before the holding thereof, in such Mode as in the Judgment of the said Board shall be sufficient to ensure Publicity. *[margin: The Matter of Schemes may be referred to an Inspector for Local Inquiry.]*

[**C. T. Act, 1853.**] **58.** Every *Inspector** to whom any such Matter shall be referred shall report in Writing to the said Board the Result of his Inquiry, and whether in his Opinion the Scheme in question should be approved with or without any Alteration or Modification thereof, and such Report shall specify or indicate the Alterations (if any) which such *Inspector** shall consider desirable, with the Reasons for the same, and also the Nature of the Objections (if any) which shall have been made to the Scheme, and the Opinion of the said *Inspector** thereon, and the said Board shall consider such Report, and if, as the Result of such Report or after further Inquiry, they shall be satisfied therewith, they may proceed to approve the Scheme in question either with or without any Alteration, and to certify the same in manner herein-after mentioned. *[margin: Inspectors to report the Result of the Inquiry to the Board.]*

[**C. T. Act, 1853.**] **59.** Every Scheme to be approved by the said Board shall be certified by them, and for that Purpose shall be embodied in a Certificate to be made by the said Board, and sealed with their Seal; and in every Case a Copy of such Certificate shall be deposited in some convenient Place within the Parish or One of the Parishes or the District in which the Charity in question shall wholly or partially be situated or administered, and at *the Office in London of the Registrar of County Courts Judgments*, and a Notice shall also be given, in such Manner as the Board shall direct, which Notice shall refer to the Certificate so deposited, and shall state the Intention of the Board to proceed with the Scheme thereby certified. *[margin: Schemes... to be... to be... and Notice given.]*

[**C. T. Act, 1855.**] **43.** The . . . . Fifty-ninth Section(s) of the principal Act shall be construed and operate as if the Words " The Office of the Board " had been inserted therein in the Place of the Words " the Office in London of the Registrar of County Courts Judgments." *[margin: Construction of Sects. 55. and 59. of 16 & 17 Vict. c. 137.]*

[*This section is printed in full at p. 72.*]

[**C. T. Act, 1853.**] **60.** The said Board shall in the Month of February in every Year make a Report to Her Majesty of all their Proceedings during the preceding Year up to the Thirty-first Day of December then last past, and such Report shall, within Fourteen Days after the making thereof, be laid before both Houses of Parliament, if Parliament be then sitting, or otherwise within Fourteen Days after the Meeting thereof; and in such Report the said Board shall specially distinguish and set forth in full all the Schemes (if any) approved by them under the Provisions lastly hereinbefore contained, together with the Grounds of such their Approval, and the Objections (if any) which have been made thereto, and all Proceedings had in respect of such Objections and the Grounds on which any such Objections have been over-ruled ; and in case it shall be enacted by any Act of Parliament that any such Scheme or Schemes so certified shall be confirmed and *[margin: Annual Report to be laid before Parliament, which shall set forth all the Schemes approved.]*

[* *Now "Assistant Commissioner," or "Assistant Commissioners," as context may require. See the Charitable Trusts Act, 1887, sect. 2, subsect. 3 (p. 13).*]

take effect, either with or without any Alterations or Modifications thereof respectively, every such Act shall be deemed a Public General Act.

(b.) *SCHEMES ESTABLISHED BY THE CHARITY COMMISSIONERS.*

Certain administrative Powers to be exercisable by the Charity Commissioners.

C. T. Act, 1860.] **2.** The Board of Charity Commissioners for England and Wales, subject to the Restrictions and Rights of Appeal herein-after provided, shall have Power from Time to Time, upon the Application of any Person or Persons who, under the Forty-third Section of "The Charitable Trusts Act, 1853," might be authorized to apply to any Judge or Court for the like Purposes, to make such effectual Orders as may now be made by any Judge of the Court of Chancery sitting at Chambers, or by any County Court *or District Court of Bankruptcy** . . . . for the Establishment of any Scheme for the Administration of any such Charity.†

[This section is printed in full in Appendix, No. 1, p. 75.]

By whom Applications may be made.

[C. T. Act, 1853.] **43.** Every Application to any Judge or Court under the Jurisdiction created or conferred by any of the Provisions of this Act, may be made by Her Majesty's Attorney General, or, subject to the Provisions aforesaid, by all or any One or more of the Trustees or Persons administering or claiming to administer, or interested in, the Charity which shall be the Subject of such Application, or any Two or more Inhabitants of any Parish or Place within which the Charity is administered or applicable ;
. . . .

[This section is printed in full in Appendix, No. 1, p. 74.]

The Powers to be exercisable over no Charities of which the gross Income shall exceed 50l. without Application of Trustees.

[C. T. Act, 1860.] **4.** The said Board shall not make any Order, under the Jurisdiction vested in them by this Act, with respect to any Charity of which the gross annual Income, exclusively of the yearly Value of any Buildings or Land used wholly for the Purposes thereof, and not yielding any pecuniary Income, shall amount to Fifty Pounds or upwards, except upon the Application of the Trustees or Persons acting in the Administration of the Charity, or a Majority of them, to be made to the said Board in Writing under their Hands if they shall be unincorporated, or under their Common Seal if they shall be incorporated, ...

[This section is printed in full in Appendix, No. 1, p. 75.]

Mode of application to Board.

[C. T. Act, 1869.] **5.** An application to the Board of Charity Commissioners for England and Wales, for the purposes of the Charitable Trusts Acts, 1853 to 1869, when made by the trustees or persons acting in the administration of the charity, may be made in writing signed by any person authorised in that behalf by a resolution passed by a majority of those trustees or persons who are present at a meeting of their body duly constituted and vote on the question.

Powers to be applicable to Charities vested in Corporations, &c

[C. T. Act, 1860.] **10.** The Jurisdiction vested by this Act in the said Board shall be exercisable with reference to Charities vested in any Corporation Sole or Aggregate, who, either solely or jointly with any other Person or Persons, shall also be the Recipients of the Benefit thereof.

Extension of part of Acts to registered places of religious worship.

[C. T. Act, 1869.] **15.** So much of the Charitable Trusts Acts, 1853, to 1869, as authorises and relates to orders of the Board . . . . for the establishment of any scheme for the administration of any charity, shall extend to buildings registered as places of meeting for religious worship with the Registrar General of Births, Deaths, or Marriages in England, and bonâ fide used as places of meeting for religious worship : Provided that no such order shall be made except upon the application of the trustees or persons acting in the administration of the Charity, made in manner provided by section four of the Charitable Trusts Act, 1860,‡ or by this Act.§ Save as

---

[* *Repealed by the Statute Law Revision Act,* 1875 (38 & 39 *Vict. c* 66.).]
† *For the jurisdiction under the Charitable Trusts Acts* (1) *of a Judge of the Chancery Division of the High Court of Justice at Chambers, see p.* 61 : (2) *of the Chancery Court of the County Palatine of Lancaster, see p.* 64 : *and* (3) *of the County Courts, see p.* 65.]
[‡ *See supra.*]   [§ *Sect. 5, supra.*]

provided by this section, such buildings shall continue exempted from the Charitable Trusts Acts, 1853 to 1869.

[This section is printed in full at p. 12.]

[C. T. Act, 1894.] 4. The exemption of any building registered as a place of meeting for religious worship with the Registrar-General of Births, Deaths, or Marriages in England and Wales, and bonâ fide used as a place of meeting for religious worship, contained in the sixty-second section of the Charitable Trusts Act, 1853, and in the ninth section of the Places of Worship Registration Act, 1855, shall extend, and shall, without prejudice to any order of the Charity Commissioners made before the passing of this Act, be deemed to have always extended to— *(margin: Extension of exemption in 16 & 17 Vict. c. 137, s. 62, 18 & 19 Vict. c. 81, s. 9, of places of meeting for religious worship.)*

    (*a*) any forecourt, yard, garden, burial ground, vestry, or caretaker's house, in respect of situation connected with, and held upon the same trusts as, any building registered and bonâ fide used as aforesaid ; and

    (*b*) any Sunday-school house or other land or building which shall be certified by an order of the Charity Commissioners, made upon the application of one or more of the trustees or persons acting in the administration thereof, to be held upon the same trusts as any building registered and used as aforesaid, or upon like trusts, and to be in respect of situation so connected with or held or used in connexion with such building that it cannot conveniently be separated therefrom :

Provided always that so much of the Charitable Trusts Acts, 1853 to 1891, as by virtue of the fifteenth section of the Charitable Trusts Act, 1869, extends to buildings registered and used as aforesaid, shall also extend to the properties declared to be exempted by this Act in the same manner and subject to the same restrictions as the buildings registered and used as aforesaid. *(margin: 32 & 33 Vict. c. 110, s. 15.)*

[C. T. Act, 1853.] 46. Nothing herein contained shall diminish or detract from any Right or Privilege which by any Rule or Practice of the Court of Chancery, or by the Construction of Law, now subsists for the Preference or the exclusive or special Benefit of the Church of England, or the Members of the same Church, in settling any Scheme for the Regulation of any Charity, [or in the Appointment or Removal of Trustees, or generally in the Application or Management of any Charity]. *(margin: Reservation of Right and Privileges of Church of England with respect to Charities.)*

[C. T. Act, 1860.] 5. The said Board also shall not exercise the Jurisdiction hereby vested in them in any Case which, by reason of its Contentious Character, or of any special Questions of Law or of Fact which it may involve, or for other Reasons, they may consider more fit to be adjudicated on by any of the Judicial Courts. *(margin: The Board shall not exercise Jurisdiction over Contentious Cases.)*

[C. T. Act, 1860.] 3. The said Board, previously to making any Order under the Jurisdiction vested in them by this Act, shall notify to the Trustees or Administrators (if any) of the Charity to be affected thereby their Intention of exercising such Jurisdiction, by Notice in Writing, to be delivered to them, or sent to them by the Post at their last known Place of Abode in Great Britain or Ireland. *(margin: Board to notify to Trustees of Charity their Intention of exercising Jurisdiction.)*

[C. T. Act, 1869.] 4. A notice under section three of the Charitable Trusts Act, 1860, need not be sent by the Board of Charity Commissioners for England and Wales to any trustee or administrator of a charity who has been party or privy to the application to the Board upon which they exercise their jurisdiction. *(margin: Amendment of s. 3 of 23 & 24 Vict. c. 136.)*

[C. T. Act, 1860.] 6. No Order . . . . establishing a Scheme for the Administration of any Charity, shall be made by the said Board before the Expiration of One Calendar Month after public Notice of the Proposal to make such Order shall have been given, as they may consider most expedient and effectual for ensuring the Publicity thereof, in each *(margin: Notices to be given of Objections and others or Suggestions to be received.)*

Parish or District in which the Charity, if of a local Character, shall be applicable, or among all Persons interested therein;   .   .   .   .   ; and every Notice hereby required shall contain (so far as conveniently may be) sufficient Particulars of the Objects of the proposed Order, and shall prescribe a reasonable Time within which any Objections thereto or Suggestions thereon may be made or transmitted to the Board; and the said Board shall receive and consider all such Objections and Suggestions, and may withhold, suspend, or modify their proposed Order, as they shall thereupon, or in the Result of further Inquiry, or otherwise, think expedient.

This section is printed in full in Appendix, No. 1, p. 75.]

Local Government Act, 1894 (56 & 57 Vict. c. 73.).] 14.—(5.) The draft of any scheme relating to a charity, not being an ecclesiastical charity, which affects a rural parish, shall, on or before the publication of the notice of the proposal to make an order for such scheme in accordance with section six of the Charitable Trusts Act, 1860, be communicated to the council of the parish, and where there is no parish council, to the chairman of the parish meeting, and, in the case of a council, the council may, subject to the provisions of this Act with respect to restrictions on expenditure, and to the consent of the parish meeting, either support or oppose the scheme, and shall for that purpose have the same right as any inhabitants of a place directly affected by the scheme.

[C. T. Act, 1869.] 7. Nothing in the Charitable Trusts Acts, 1853 to 1869, shall be deemed to require or to have required the Board, upon modifying a proposed order in manner provided by section six of the Charitable Trusts Act, 1860, after the publication thereof, to give public notice of such modified order in the manner provided by that section with respect to the order originally proposed, unless they think further notice desirable.

[C. T. Act, 1860.] 7. A Copy of every such Order when made shall, in the Case of any local Charity, be deposited for the Space of One Calendar Month in some convenient Place within the Parish or One of the Parishes or in the District in which the Charity shall be applicable, and shall be open to public Inspection there at all reasonable Hours during the same Period; and a Copy also   very such Order relating to any Charity, whether local or general, shall be kept, open to public Inspection at all reasonable Hours, at the Office of the Commissioners, during a like period of One Calendar Month; and in each Case effectual Publicity shall be given to the making of the Order by such Means as the Board shall consider most expedient for that.

[C. T. Act, 1860.] 8. The Attorney General, or any Person authorized by him or by the said Board, in the Case of any Charity, whatever may be the yearly Income of its Endowments, and any Trustee or Person acting in the Administration of or interested in any Charity of which the gross yearly Income to be calculated in manner aforesaid* shall exceed Fifty Pounds, or any Two inhabitants of any Parish or District in which the same shall be specially applicable, may, within Three Calendar Months next after the definitive Publication of any Order of the said Board   .   .   . establishing a Scheme for the Administration of the Charity, present a Petition to the High Court of Chancery in a summary Way, appealing against such Order, and praying such Relief as the Case may require   .   .   . ; and the Court, upon or before the Hearing of any such Petition of Appeal as aforesaid or at any Stage of the Proceedings, may require, if it shall think fit, from the said Board, their Reasons for making the Order appealed against, or for any part of such Order, and may remit the same to the Board for Reconsideration, with or without any Declaration in relation thereto, or may make any substitutive or other Order in relation to the Matter of the Appeal, as it shall think just; and the Court may make any Order respecting the Costs, Charges, or Expenses incident to the Appeal, and may also, before hearing or proceeding with the same, require from any Appellant, other than the Attorney General, proper Security for such Costs, Charges, and Expenses as may be eventually payable by him; but no such

[* See sect. 4 of the Charitable Trusts Act, 1860, (p. 54).]

Petition of Appeal shall be presented by any Person, other than the Attorney General, before the Expiration of Twenty-one Days after written Notice, under the Hand of such Appellant, of his or her Intention to present such Petition, shall have been delivered to the said Board at their Office.

[*This section is printed in full in Appendix, No. 1, p. 75.*]

[C. T. Act, 1869.] 10. A petition to the Court of Chancery under section eight of the Charitable Trusts Act, 1860, may be presented in the case of all charities by the same persons only as in the case of a charity the gross annual income of which does not exceed fifty pounds. *Appeal under 23 & 24 Vict. c. 136.*

[C. T. Act, 1869.] 11. A petition shall not be presented to the Court of Chancery by any person under section eight of the Charitable Trusts Act, 1860, before the expiration of twenty-one days after written notice under the hand of the appellant of his intention to present such petition has been served on the Attorney-General by delivering the same to the solicitor who acts for him in ex officio proceedings relating to charities. *Service of Attorney General by appellant under sect. 8 of 23 & 24 Vict. c. 136.*

[C. T. Act, 1860.] 9. The Attorney General, if he shall think fit, or any Person authorized by him or by the said Board, may appear as the Respondent upon any such Appeal, and the Court may make any Order respecting the Costs, Charges, and Expenses of the Attorney General or other Defendant. *Who may be the Respondent on Appeals.*

[C. T. Act, 1869.] 9. The Board, if they think it desirable, where the gross annual income of a charity is in their opinion sufficient to bear the expense, may, upon the application of the trustees or of any other person or persons entitled to apply to them in that behalf, employ or may authorise the trustees or persons acting in the administration of such charity to employ skilled and competent persons to prepare any scheme, order, statement, or other proceeding for the purposes of the Charitable Trusts Acts, 1853 to 1869, with respect to such charity, or to make or assist in any survey or local inquiry with reference thereto, and may order the costs incurred under this section or upon any inquiry by an *inspector*,* or in consequence of the employment of any person to appear on behalf of the respondent upon any appeal against any scheme or order, to be provided in the same manner as if they were costs of a transaction mentioned in section thirty-six of the Charitable Trusts Act, 1855.† *Employment of persons to prepare and defend scheme.*

(c.) *ORDERS MADE BY THE CHARITY COMMISSIONERS FOR THE APPORTIONMENT OF CHARITIES.*

[C. T. Act, 1855.] 10. Where any Parish or Ecclesiastical District entitled to the Benefit of a Charity has or shall have been divided into separate Parishes or Ecclesiastical Districts, and no Apportionment of Charities originally applicable to the Parish or District so divided shall have been made by Parliament or other competent Authority, the Board, in respect of all Charities the gross annual Income whereof does not for the Time being exceed Thirty Pounds, may apportion the Benefit of the Charity between each new Parish or District, or any Portion thereof taken from the Parish or District originally entitled to the whole Benefit, and the Remainder of such last-mentioned Parish or District, in such Manner and such Proportions as, upon a Consideration of the Purposes of the Charity, the Population of each Parish or District, and other Circumstances, they may think fit, and may also apportion the principal Endowments between such Parishes or Districts, if it be thought fit, and may appoint separate Trustees of any Part of the Endowments. *Power to apportion Parochial Charities after Division of Parishes.*

[C. T. Act, 1855.] 11. The Certificate of the Board, that according to their Judgment the gross yearly Income of the Charity does not for the *Evidence as to annual Income of*

[* *Now "Assistant Commissioner." See Charitable Trusts Act, 1887, sect. 2, subs. 3. (p. 13).*]
[† *For this section, see p. 29.*]

any Charity not exceeding 50l. — Time being exceed Thirty Pounds, shall be sufficient Evidence of the Amount of such annual Income for the Purpose of determining the Jurisdiction under the foregoing Provision.

Notices to be given of certain Orders of the Board. — **[C. T. Act, 1855.]** 13. No Order for apportioning the Benefits of any Charity shall be made by the Board until after such public Notices shall have been given of the Proposal to make the same as the Board may consider expedient for insuring Publicity in each Parish or District in which the Charity is or ought to be applied, or among all Persons interested therein, nor until after the Expiration of One Month from the Publication of such Notice; and every such Notice shall contain (so far as conveniently may be) sufficient Particulars of the proposed Order to show the Objects thereof, and shall prescribe a Time within which any Objections thereto may be stated or transmitted to the Board.

Proceedings upon the Receipt of Objections or Suggestions — **[C. T. Act, 1855.]** 14. All Objections which may be made to any proposed Order shall be considered by the Board, who may suspend the making thereof for further Inquiry, or may modify the same, as may be found expedient; and a Copy of every such Order when made shall, in the Case of any local Charity, be deposited for the Space of One Month in some convenient Place within the Parish or One of the Parishes or the District in which the Charity is applicable, and also be open to Inspection at the Office of the Commissioners, and such Publicity shall be given thereto among all Persons interested in the Charity as the Board shall consider expedient; or if the Charity be not local then a Copy of such Order shall be open to Inspection at the Office of the Commissioners, and public Notice thereof shall be given in such Manner as to the Board shall seem fit, and in Cases where there is a special Visitor, Notice shall be given to him.

XI.—Amendments of Legal Procedure and Creation of Summary Jurisdiction over Charities.

(a.) INSTITUTION BY THE CHARITY COMMISSIONERS, IN THE NAME OF THE BOARD, OF LEGAL PROCEEDINGS FOR THE RECOVERY OF PROPERTY BELONGING TO CHARITIES.

Interpretation. — [C. T. Act, 1891.] 2. In this Act, unless the context requires otherwise,—

The expression "the Board" means the Charity Commissioners for England and Wales:

The expression "prescribed" means prescribed by rules made under the provisions of this Act.

Power to Board to sue for recovery of property belonging to charities. — **[C. T. Act, 1891.]** 3. Where it appears to the Board that any action, petition, or other proceeding should be instituted for the recovery of any property, the gross annual income of which does not, in the opinion of the Board, exceed twenty pounds a year, and which appears to the Board to belong to a charity, the Board may itself, with the sanction of the Attorney General, institute such proceeding on behalf of the Charity; and the expenses of the Board of and incidental to such action, petition, or proceeding shall be paid in like manner as if they were costs of the Attorney General in a charity matter.

Mode of procedure by Board. — **[C. T. Act, 1891.]** 4.—(1.) When the Board is authorised to make any application to or appear in any court, or to institute any action, petition, or other proceeding, such application or appearance may be made, and such action, petition, or proceeding may be instituted, in the name of the Charity

Commissioners for England and Wales, and not in the names of the persons who are the Commissioners.

(2.) Any action, petition, application, appearance, or other proceeding instituted or made by the Board shall not abate or become defective by reason of any change in the persons who are the Commissioners, but the Commissioners for the time being shall be deemed to be parties thereto.

(3.) For the purposes of any such action, petition, application, appearance, or other proceeding, any document may be served on the Board by being addressed to the Board and delivered at or sent by post to the office of the Board, or by being served on the Secretary to the Board.

(4.) Any application by the Board to the Court in pursuance of this Act may be made in manner for the time being directed by rules of court.*

[C. T. Act, 1891.] 5. For the purposes of any action, petition, or proceeding instituted by the Board under this Act the following provisions shall have effect :— *Special remedies given to Board.*

  (1.) The printed reports of the Charity Commissioners appointed under an Act passed in the fifty-eighth year of the reign of His Majesty George the Third, and intituled "An Act for appointing Commissioners to "inquire concerning charities in England for the education of the "poor," and under other Acts for inquiring into Charities, shall be admissible as primâ facie evidence of the documents and facts therein stated ; provided that either party intending to use any such report as evidence shall give notice of such intention in the prescribed manner to the other party : *Old reports of Charity Commissioners to be evidence. 58 Geo. 3. c. 91.*

  (2.) Where any yearly or other periodical payment has been made in respect of any land, to or for the benefit of any charity or charitable purpose, for twelve consecutive years, such payment shall be deemed, subject to any evidence which may be given to the contrary, primâ facie evidence of the perpetual liability of such land to such yearly or other periodical payment, and no proof of the origin of such payment shall be necessary. *Payment for twelve years to be presumptive evidence.*

[C. T. Act, 1891.] 6. Rules for practice and procedure under this Act, including fees and costs, whether in the Supreme Court of Judicature or in the county court, may from time to time be made by the authority and in the manner by and in which rules may be made for regulating the practice and procedure in such Supreme Court or county court, as the case may be.* *Rules.*

(b.) INTERVENTION OF THE CHARITY COMMISSIONERS IN THE INSTITUTION OF LEGAL PROCEEDINGS WITH RESPECT TO CHARITIES.

[C. T. Act, 1853.] 17. Before any Suit, Petition, or other Proceeding (not being an application in any Suit or Matter actually pending) for obtaining any Relief, Order or Direction, concerning or relating to any Charity, or the Estate, Funds, Property, or Income thereof, shall be commenced, presented, or taken, by any Person whomsoever, there shall be transmitted by such Person to the said Board, Notice in Writing of such proposed Suit, Petition, or Proceeding, and such Statement, Information, and Particulars as may be requisite or proper, or may be required from Time to Time, by the said Board, for explaining the Nature and Objects thereof ; and the said Board, if upon Consideration of the Circumstances they so think fit, may, by an Order or Certificate signed by their Secretary,† authorize or direct any Suit, Petition, or other Proceeding to be commenced, presented, or taken with respect to such Charity, either for the Objects and in the Manner specified or mentioned in such Notice, or for such other Objects, and in such Manner and Form, and subject to such Stipulations or Provisions *Notice of legal Proceedings as to any Charity by any Person, except the Attorney General, to be given to the Board.*

[* For rules regulating the procedure under this Act (1) in the High Court of Justice, see " The Rules of the Supreme Court (Charitable Trusts Recovery), 1892," made on 27th May 1892, and (2) in a County Court, see County Court Rules (July) 1892.]

[† But see now Charitable Trusts Amendment Act, 1855, sect. 4 (p. 16), and Charitable Trusts Act, 1887, sect. 3 (p. 16).]

for securing the Charity against Liability to any Costs or Expenses, and to such other Stipulations or Provisions for the Protection or Benefit of the Charity, as the said Board may think proper; and such Board, if it seem proper to them, may by such Order or Certificate as aforesaid require and direct that any Proceeding so authorized by them in respect of any Charity, shall be delayed during such Period as shall seem proper to and shall be directed by such Board; and every such Order or Certificate may be in such Form and may contain such Statements and Particulars as such Board shall **Courts not to entertain Proceedings as to Charities, except upon Certificate of the Board.** think fit; and (save as herein otherwise provided*) no Suit, Petition, or other Proceeding for obtaining any such Relief, Order, or Direction as last aforesaid shall be entertained or proceeded with by the Court of Chancery, or by any Court or Judge, except upon and in conformity with an Order or Certificate of the said Board: Provided always, that this Enactment shall not extend to or affect any such Petition or Proceeding in which any Person shall claim any Property or seek any Relief adversely to any Charity.

Saving for the Attorney General acting ex-officio. [**C. T. Act, 1853.**] 18. Provided always, That it shall be lawful for Her Majesty's Attorney General acting ex-officio to make such Applications, and take and prosecute such Proceedings with respect to any Charity, in the Court of Chancery or otherwise as to him may seem fit, as if this Act had not been passed; and that nothing in this Act contained shall be construed as dispensing with the Fiat or Allowance of Her Majesty's Attorney General, with respect to any Proceeding not being an Application under the Jurisdiction created by this Act† where such Fiat or Allowance was necessary before the passing of this Act.

Board may, upon the Report of an Inspector, authorize Proceedings where no Notice has been given to them, and may in other Cases cause local Inquiries by their Inspector. [**C. T. Act, 1853.**] 19. Provided also, That where upon any Report of any *Inspector‡* under this Act or otherwise it appears to the said Board that any Suit, Petition, or other Proceeding concerning or relating to any Charity, or the Estate, Funds, Property or Income thereof, would be proper or expedient, it shall be lawful for the said Board by their Order to authorize or direct such Suit, Petition, or Proceeding to be commenced, presented, or taken, and to give such Directions in relation thereto as the said Board may think proper; and thereupon such Suit, Petition, or Proceeding may be commenced, presented, or taken accordingly, without any such previous Notice in Writing as herein-before mentioned; and the said Board, before [giving any such Opinion, Advice, or Direction upon any such Application as aforesaid or] making any such Order or Certificate after Notice to them as aforesaid, may, where local Inquiry appears to them to be requisite, cause such Inquiry to be made by One of their *Inspectors* :‡ and the said Board may, in any Case where they see fit, before acting upon the Report of any *Inspector*,‡ cause such Report to be deposited for local Inspection, and give Notice of the same being so deposited, and consider any Statements or Objections which may be transmitted to them in relation thereto.

Legal proceedings by trustees of charities for protection of charity property, &c. [**C. T. Act, 1869.**] 13. The majority of the trustees of any charity, if authorised by the Board, may institute and maintain any action, suit, petition, or other proceeding in the same manner in all respects as if they were the sole trustees of the charity.

Where the trustees, or the majority of the trustees, of any charity, institute and maintain any action, suit, petition, or other proceeding under the authority of the Board, such action, suit, petition or other proceeding shall not abate or become discontinued or of no effect by reason of the death or removal from office of any of the trustees, or of the addition of any new trustee, but shall continue and have effect for and against the trustees for the time being of the charity, in the same manner as if they were actually named therein.

[* *See last paragraph of sect.* 28 (*p.* 62), *and so far as regards proceedings by the Attorney General, sects.* 18 (*infra*), 20 (*p.* 61), 28 (*p.* 61), 32 (*p.* 65), 39 (*p.* 69), 43 (*p.* 74).]

[† *For the jurisdiction conferred by the Charitable Trusts Acts* (1) *upon Judges of the Chancery Division of the High Court of Justice at Chambers, see p.* 61; (2) *upon the Court of Chancery of the County Palatine of Lancaster, see p.* 64; *and* (3) *upon the County Courts, see p.* 65.]

[‡ *Now* "*Assistant Commissioner,*" *or* "*Assistant Commissioners,*" *as context may require. See Charitable Trusts Act,* 1887, *sect.* 2, *sub-sect.* 3 (*p.* 13).]

[C. T. Act, 1853.] 20. In any Case in which it shall appear to the said Board that the Institution of legal Proceedings is requisite or desirable with respect to any Charity, or the Estates, Funds, Property, or Affairs thereof, and that under the Circumstances thereof it is desirable that such Proceedings should be instituted by the Attorney General, it shall be lawful for the said Board, if they so think fit, to certify such Case, in Writing under the Hand of the Secretary of the said Board,* to Her Majesty's Attorney General, together with such Statements and Particulars (if any) as in the Opinion of the said Board may be requisite or proper for the Explanation of such Case; and thereupon the said Attorney General, if upon Consideration of the Circumstances he think fit, shall institute and prosecute such legal Proceedings as he shall consider requisite or proper under the Circumstances of such Case, by Information,† or Petition in the Court of Chancery, or by Application to a Judge thereof at Chambers, or to a *District Court of Bankruptcy, or‡* County Court under the Jurisdiction given by this Act.§

Power for Board to certify certain Cases to the Attorney General.

(c.) *POWER TO THE ATTORNEY GENERAL TO PETITION UNDER THE CHARITIES PROCEDURE ACT, 1812.*

[C. T. Act, 1853.] 43. . . . . and it shall be lawful for Her Majesty's Attorney General for the Time being, acting ex-officio, to make Application by Petition to the Court of Chancery with respect to any Charity under the Provisions of the Act passed in the Fifty-second Year of King George the Third, Chapter One hundred and one, or under the Provisions of any Act or Acts passed or to be passed authorizing the Application to the same Court by Petition according to the Provisions of the said Act.

Attorney General may Petition under 52 G. 3. c. 101.

[*This section is printed in full in Appendix, No. 1, p. 71.*]

(d.) *SPECIAL JURISDICTION AT CHAMBERS CONFERRED UPON JUDGES OF THE CHANCERY DIVISION OF THE HIGH COURT OF JUSTICE.*

[C. T. Act, 1853.] 28. Where the Appointment or Removal of any Trustee, or any other Relief, Order, or Direction relating to any Charity of which the gross annual Income for the Time being exceeds Thirty Pounds, shall be considered desirable, and such Appointment, Removal, or other Relief, Order, or Direction might now be made or given by the Court of Chancery, in respect either of its ordinary or its special or statutory Jurisdiction, or by the Lord Chancellor intrusted with the Care and Commitment of the Custody of Lunatics, it shall be lawful for any Person authorized in this Behalf by the Order, or Certificate of the said Board, or for the Attorney General, to make Application (without any Information, Bill, or Petition,) to the Master of the Rolls‖ or One of the Vice Chancellors‖ sitting at Chambers, for such Order, Direction, or Relief as the Nature of the Case may require; and the Master of the Rolls‖ or the Vice Chancellor‖ to whom any such Application shall be made shall and may proceed upon and dispose of such Application in Chambers, save where he may think fit otherwise to direct, and shall and may have and exercise thereupon all such Jurisdiction, Power, and Authority, and make such Orders and give such Directions in relation to the Matter of such Application, as might now be exercised, made, or given by the Court of Chancery or by the Lord Chancellor intrusted as aforesaid, in a Suit regularly instituted, or upon Petition, as the Case may require; and the Master of the Rolls‖ and Vice Chancellors‖ respectively shall, in relation to such Applications as aforesaid, and the Proceedings thereon, (subject to any Rules which may be made by the Lord Chancellor,

In Cases of Charities the Incomes of which exceed 30l., the Rolls and Vice Chancellors, upon Applications to them at Chambers, to have the same Jurisdiction as the Court of Chancery or Lord Chancellor now has upon Information, &c.

[* *But see now Charitable Trusts Amendment Act, 1855, sect. 4. (p. 16), and Charitable Trusts Act, 1887, sect. 3 (p. 16).*]
[† *Now "action." Rules of the Supreme Court, 1883, Order 1, Rule 1.*]
[‡ *Repealed by the Statute Law Revision Act, 1875 (38 & 39 Vict. c. 66).*]
[§ *For the jurisdiction under the Charitable Trusts Acts (1) of Judges of the Chancery Division of the High Court of Justice at Chambers, see infra; (2) of the Court of Chancery of the County Palatine of Lancaster, see p. 64; and (3) of the County Courts, see p. 65.*]
[‖ *The jurisdiction under this section is now by virtue of the Judicature Act, 1873, sects. 16, 34, and 76, exercised by the Judges of the Chancery Division of the High Court of Justice.*]

H 3

with the Advice and Consent of them or any Two of them,) have all such Powers of directing Matters to be heard in open Court, and of ordering what Matters shall be heard and investigated by themselves and their Chief Clerks respectively, and such other Powers and Authorities as by the Act of the last Session of Parliament, Chapter Eighty, are vested in or authorized to be exercised by them at Chambers* and the Provisions of the said Act applicable to Orders made by the Master of the Rolls or any of the Vice Chancellors at Chambers shall extend to all Orders so made under this Act : Provided always, that, save as may be otherwise provided by any Rules to be made by the Lord Chancellor, with such Advice and Consent as aforesaid, the Determinations of the Master of the Rolls and Vice Chancellors respectively upon and in relation to such Applications as aforesaid shall not be subject to Appeal in any Case where the gross annual Income of the Charity does not exceed One hundred Pounds :† Provided also, that it shall be lawful for the Master of the Rolls or any Vice Chancellor, where under the Circumstances of any Application as aforesaid he may so see fit, to direct that for obtaining the Relief, Order, or Direction sought for by such Application an Information, Bill, or Petition, as the case may require, shall be filed or presented and prosecuted as now by Law required, and to abstain from further Proceeding on such Application.

Provisions as to Charities exceeding 30l. per Annum to extend to Charities in London not exceeding 30l.

[C. T. Act, 1853.] 30. Provided always, That the Provisions of this Act applicable to any Charity the gross annual Income whereof exceeds Thirty Pounds shall extend to any Charity established or administered or applicable to or for Objects or Purposes within the City of London the gross annual Income whereof does not exceed Thirty Pounds, in like Manner as if such Income exceeded that Amount.

Board may direct Cases within the Jurisdiction of a District or County Court to be taken before a Judge of the Court of Chancery in the first instance.

[C. T. Act, 1853.] 35. It shall be lawful for the said Board to direct that any Application as to any Charity within the Jurisdiction of any *District Court of Bankruptcy or‡* County Court§ shall be made before a Judge of the Court of Chancery, or as to any Charity within the Jurisdiction of the Court of Chancery of the County Palatine of Lancaster, either before the Chancellor or the Vice Chancellor of the same County Palatine, or before a Judge of the High Court of Chancery, according to the Provisions herein contained applicable to a Charity the gross annual Income whereof exceeds Thirty Pounds, and in such Case such Application shall be made and may be heard and determined accordingly, in like Manner as if the gross annual Income of such Charity exceeded Thirty Pounds ; and upon the Production of the Order or Certificate containing such Direction, or of a Copy thereof, the Application with respect to which such Order or Certificate shall have been made shall not be entertained or proceeded with by such *District or‡* County Court.

Board, if dissatisfied with the Order of District or County Court may remit the Case for Reconsideration, or may transfer the Matter to a Judge of the Court of Chancery.

[C. T. Act, 1853.] 37. In case any such Order or Decision as last aforesaid of any *District Court of Bankruptcy or‡* County Court shall not be approved by the said Board, it shall be lawful for such Board to remit the same for Reconsideration and Decision by such *District or‡* County Court, with such Remarks and Recommendations thereon (if any) as shall seem fit and expedient to such Board, or, in the Discretion of the Board, to order, and direct that the Subject Matter to which such Order or Decision relates, together with such Order or Decision, shall be submitted to the Consideration and Decision of a Judge of the Court of Chancery, and in such last-mentioned Case no further Proceedings shall be had or taken in the *District or‡* County Court with respect to the Matter in question ; and in case the Order or Decision of the *District or‡* County Court, on the Reconsideration of any Order or Decision so remitted for Reconsideration, be disapproved as aforesaid by the said Board, such Board shall refer such Orders and Decisions,

---

[* *The business in Chambers of the Judges of the Chancery Division is now regulated by the Rules of the Supreme Court, 1883, Order 55, and the greater part of the Act referred to (Master in Chancery Abolition Act, 1852) is now repealed.*]

[† *With regard to appeals, see now Rules of the Supreme Court 1883, Order 55, Rule 14.*]

[‡ *Repealed by the Statute Law Revision Act, 1892 (55 & 56 Vict. c. 19.).*]

[§ *For the jurisdiction of the County Courts, see p. 65.*]

and the Subject Matter thereof, to a Judge of the Court of Chancery, or, as to any Charity within the Jurisdiction of the Court of Chancery of the County Palatine of Lancaster, either to the Chancellor or the Vice Chancellor of the same County Palatine, or to a Judge of the High Court of Chancery; and where any Order or Decision is referred to a Judge of the Court of Chancery, or of the Court of Chancery of the said County Palatine of Lancaster, under this Provision, such Judge shall have and exercise all such Jurisdiction, Power, and Authority in relation thereto as in the Case of a Charity the gross annual Income whereof exceeds Thirty Pounds, and may make such Order in relation to the Matter of such Order or Decision as to him may seem proper.

[C. T. Act, 1853.] 41. Provided always, That no Judge of the Court of Chancery, ... shall upon any Proceedings under this Act have Jurisdiction to try or determine the Title at Law or in Equity to any real or Personal Property, or any Term or Interest therein, as between any Charity, or the Trustee thereof, and any Person holding or claiming such Real or Personal Property, Term, or Interest adversely to such Charity, or to try or determine any Question as to the Existence or Extent of any Charge or Trust. *[side note: No Chancery Judge, or District or County Court, in Proceedings under this Act to try Titles, &c.]*

[*This section is printed in full in Appendix, No. 1, p. 74.*]

[C. T. Act, 1853.] 46. Nothing herein contained shall diminish or detract from any Right or Privilege which by any Rule or Practice of the Court of Chancery, or by the Construction of Law, now subsists for the Preference or the exclusive or special Benefit of the Church of England, or the Members of the same Church, in settling any Scheme for the Regulation of any Charity, or in the Appointment or Removal of Trustees, or generally in the Application or Management of any Charity. *[side note: Reservation of Rights and Privileges of Church of England with respect to Charities.]*

[Endowed Schools Act, 1874 (37 & 38 Vict. c. 87).] 6. The powers of making schemes under the Endowed Schools Acts as amended by this Act shall continue in force for a period of five years from the said thirty-first day of December one thousand eight hundred and seventy-four;* and during the continuance of such powers any court or judge shall not, with respect to any endowed school or educational endowment which can be dealt with by a scheme under this Act and the Endowed Schools Acts, or any of such Acts, make any scheme or appoint any new trustees without the consent of the Committee of Council on Education. *[side note: Continuance of powers transferred to Charity Commissioners.]*

[C. T. Act, 1853.] 44. For the Purposes of determining the Jurisdiction under this Act with respect to any Charity, or the right to appeal from the Determination of a Judge of the Court of Chancery, it shall be lawful for the said Board to declare, according to such Judgment as they may be able to form upon the Returns or Statements before them in relation to any Charity, whether the gross annual Income for the Time being of such Charity does or does not exceed Thirty Pounds† or One hundred Pounds, (as the Case may require,) and a Statement in any Certificate or Order of the said Board that according to such Judgment as aforesaid the gross yearly Income of any Charity does or does not exceed Thirty Pounds† or One hundred Pounds shall be sufficient Evidence of the Amount of the gross annual Income of such Charity, for the Purpose of determining such Jurisdiction or Right to appeal as aforesaid; and any Certificate or Order made by the said Board under this Act, authorizing any Proceeding or Application concerning any Charity to be taken or made to any *District Court of Bankruptcy* or‡ to the Court of Chancery or any Judge thereof, shall state that the gross annual Income for the Time being of such Charity does not exceed Thirty† Pounds, or does exceed Thirty† Pounds (as the case may be): Provided always, that where any Charity, of *[side note: Statement in Certificate of Board of the Amount of Income of any Charity to be sufficient Evidence for determining the Jurisdiction or Proceedings under this Act.]*

[* These powers were continued up to 31st March 1898, by sect. 1, sub-sect. 2, of Expiring Laws Continuance Act, 1896, (59 & 60 Vict. c. 39).]
[† The increase of the limit of the County Court jurisdiction under the Charitable Trusts Acts from 30l. to 50l. (C. T. Act, 1860, s. 11, p. 67) has not affected the jurisdiction of the Judges of the Chancery Division in Chambers over any Charity the gross income of which exceeds 30l. but is less than 50l.]
[‡ Repealed by the Statute Law Revision Act, 1892 (55 & 56 Vict. c. 19).]

Proviso as to particular Endowments
the Trustees thereof, in addition to the principal Endowment for its general Objects and Purposes, shall be possessed of or entitled to any other Endowment for any particular or special Object or Purpose arising out of or in its Nature or Application connected with the general Objects or Purposes of such Charity, it shall be lawful for the said Board, having regard to the circumstances of each such Case, and to the Object and Extent of the proposed Application and Litigation, to determine whether such Endowment for such particular or special Object or Purpose should, for the Purposes of Jurisdiction and Proceedings under this Act, be considered and treated as forming Part of the general Endowment of the Charity, or as a separate or independent Charity, and such Board shall frame their Certificate or Order accordingly.

By whom Applications may be made.
[C. T. Act, 1853.] 43. Every application to any Judge or Court under the Jurisdiction created or conferred by any of the Provisions of this Act, may be made by Her Majesty's Attorney General, or, subject to the Provisions aforesaid, by all or any One or more of the Trustees or Persons administering or claiming to administer, or interested in, the Charity which shall be the Subject of such Application, or any Two or more Inhabitants of any Parish or Place within which the Charity is administered or applicable;

. . . .

[This section is printed in full in Appendix, No. 1, p. 74.]

Notice to be published of Application for Schemes or Appointment or Removal of Trustees under this Act.
[C. T. Act, 1853.] 42. Before any Application shall be made to any Judge of the Court of Chancery, ... under any of the Provisions herein contained for the Establishment or Alteration of a Scheme or the Appointment or Removal of any Trustees or Trustee, Notice in Writing of such intended Application shall be given in such Form and Manner as the said Board shall have directed; and if the Order be that such Notice be affixed to or near the Door of any Parish or District Church, the Incumbent and Churchwardens of such Parish or District are hereby respectively required to allow such Notice to be affixed and to remain so affixed during such Period, not less than Fifteen Days, as the said Board shall have ordered; and in any Case in which the Order shall be that such Notice shall be affixed to any Place, Evidence that the same has been so affixed shall be deemed and taken as primâ facie Evidence that it has remained affixed during the Period prescribed by the Board.

[This section is printed in full in Appendix, No. 1, p. 74.]

Lord Chancellor, with the Advice of Master of the Rolls and Vice Chancellors, or Two of them, to make General Orders.
[C. T. Act, 1853.] 31. It shall be lawful for the Lord Chancellor, with the Advice and Consent of the Master of the Rolls and Vice Chancellors, or any Two of them, to make and issue General Rules and Orders for regulating the Mode and Form of Applications at the Chambers of the Master of the Rolls and Vice Chancellors respectively under this Act, and the Proceedings thereon, and for determining in what Cases and under what Conditions and Restrictions the Determinations of the Master of the Rolls and Vice Chancellors respectively upon or in relation to such Applications shall be subject to Appeal, and the Fees and Allowances to Solicitors of the Court of Chancery, and the Fees to be payable in Money or by Stamps to the Officers of the said Court in respect of such Applications and Proceedings thereon; and such Rules and Orders may from Time to Time be varied by the like Authority, and all such Rules and Orders shall be deemed General Orders of the said Court.*

(e.) *SPECIAL JURISDICTION CONFERRED UPON THE COURT OF CHANCERY OF THE COUNTY PALATINE OF LANCASTER.*

Provision as to Charities within the
[C. T. Act, 1853.] 29. The Jurisdiction created and given by this Act to the Master of the Rolls and the Vice Chancellors sitting in Chambers,† upon

[* *See footnotes on p. 61 and * on p. 62. With regard to appeals, see now Rules of the Supreme Court, 1883, Order 55, Rule 14, and with regard to costs, see Order 65, Rules 24 and 25.*]
[† *See ante, p. 61.*]

any Application to them respectively as aforesaid, shall extend concurrently to and may be exercised by the Chancellor of the Duchy and County Palatine of Lancaster, and the Vice Chancellor of the same County Palatine respectively for the Time being, as to every Charity within the Jurisdiction of the Court of Chancery of the said County Palatine whose gross annual Income for the Time being exceeds Thirty Pounds, upon Application being made to such Chancellor or Vice Chancellor respectively; and it shall be lawful for the Chancellor of the said Duchy and County Palatine, with the Concurrence of the Vice Chancellor of the same County Palatine, from Time to Time to make and issue any Rules and Orders for regulating the modes of proceeding, and the Fees to be taken in respect of Proceedings under this Act. *{Jurisdiction of the Court of Chancery of the County Palatine of Lancaster.}*

[C. T. Act, 1853]. 35. It shall be lawful for the said Board to direct that any Application as to any Charity within the Jurisdiction of any *District Court of Bankruptcy or** County Courts† shall be made as to any Charity within the Jurisdiction of the Court of Chancery of the County Palatine of Lancaster, either before the Chancellor or the Vice Chancellor of the same County Palatine, or before a Judge of the High Court of Chancery, according to the Provisions herein contained applicable to a Charity the gross annual Income whereof exceeds Thirty Pounds, and in such Case such Application shall be made and may be heard and determined accordingly, in like Manner as if the gross annual Income of such Charity exceeded Thirty Pounds; and upon the Production of the Order or Certificate containing such Direction, or of a Copy thereof, the Application with respect to which such Order or Certificate shall have been made shall not be entertained or proceeded with by such *District or** County Court. *{Board may direct Cases within the Jurisdiction of a District or County Court to be taken before a Judge of the Court of Chancery in the first instance.}*

[C. T. Act, 1853.] 37. In case any such Order or Decision as last aforesaid of any *District Court of Bankruptcy or** County Court shall not be approved by the said Board, it shall be lawful for such Board to remit the same for Reconsideration and Decision by such *District or** County Court, with such Remarks and Recommendations thereon (if any) as shall seem fit and expedient to such Board, or, in the Discretion of the Board, to order, and direct that the Subject Matter to which such Order or Decision relates, together with such Order or Decision, shall be submitted to the Consideration and Decision of a Judge of the Court of Chancery, and in such last-mentioned Case no further Proceedings shall be had or taken in the *District or** County Court with respect to the Matter in question; and in case the Order or Decision of the *District or** County Court, on the Reconsideration of any Order or Decision so remitted for Reconsideration, be disapproved as aforesaid by the said Board, such Board shall refer such Orders and Decisions, and the Subject Matter thereof, to a Judge of the Court of Chancery, or, as to any Charity within the Jurisdiction of the Court of Chancery of the County Palatine of Lancaster, either to the Chancellor or the Vice Chancellor of the same County Palatine, or to a Judge of the High Court of Chancery; and where any Order or Decision is referred to a Judge of the Court of Chancery, or of the Court of Chancery of the said County Palatine of Lancaster, under this Provision, such Judge shall have and exercise all such Jurisdiction, Power, and Authority in relation thereto as in the Case of a Charity the gross annual Income whereof exceeds Thirty Pounds, and may make such Order in relation to the Matter of such Order or Decision as to him may seem proper. *{Board, if dissatisfied with the Order of District or County Court may remit the Case for Reconsideration, or may transfer the Matter to a Judge of the Court of Chancery.}*

have Juris-
diction in
Cases of
Charities the
Incomes of
which do
not exceed
30*l.*

or Purposes within the District or any Two or more of the Districts *of any District Court of Bankruptcy or** of any County Court or Courts *holden under the Act of the Session holden in the Ninth and Tenth Years of the reign of Her Majesty, Chapter Ninety-five,** and the Appointment or Removal of any Trustee, or any other Relief, Order, or Direction whatsoever concerning such Charity, shall be considered desirable, and such Appointment or Removal, or other Relief, Order, or Direction, might now be made or given by the Court of Chancery in respect either of its ordinary or its special or statutory Jurisdiction, or by the Lord Chancellor intrusted with the Care and Commitment of the Custody of Lunatics, it shall be lawful for any Person authorized in this Behalf by the Order or Certificate of the said Board, or for the Attorney-General, to make Application to such *District or** County Court, or, as the Case may be, to any one of such *District or** County Courts, for such Order, Direction, or Relief as the Nature of the Case may require; and such *District or** County Court shall entertain such Application, and shall hear the Matter in open Court, and shall give such Relief, and make such Orders and Directions in relation to the Matter of such Application, as might now be made or given by the Court of Chancery or by the Lord Chancellor, intrusted as aforesaid, in a suit regularly instituted, or upon Petition, as the Case may require; and the Clerk of such County Court† shall transmit a Copy of such Order or Direction to the Office in London of the Registrar of County Courts Judgments, to be there enrolled; Provided always, that no Judge of any *District or** County Court shall be authorized to vary any Decree, Order, or Direction of the Court of Chancery, or of any Judge thereof, or to make or give any Order or Direction inconsistent or conflicting with any such Decree, Order, or Direction: Provided also, that where Two or more *District or** County Courts shall have concurrent Jurisdiction with respect to any Charity under this Act, no Application in respect of such Charity shall be made to or entertained by more than One of such *District or** County Courts at the same Time.

No Chancery Judge, or District or County Court, in Proceedings under this Act to try Titles, &c.

[C. T. Act, 1853.]　41. Provided always, That no . . . . *District Court of Bankruptcy or** County Court, shall upon any Proceedings under this Act have Jurisdiction to try or determine the Title at Law or in Equity to any Real or Personal Property, or any Term or Interest therein, as between any Charity, or the Trustee thereof, and any Person holding or claiming such Real or Personal Property, Term, or Interest adversely to such Charity, or to try or determine any Question as to the Existence or Extent of any Charge or Trust.

[This section is printed in full in Appendix, No. 1, p. 74.]

Reservation of Rights and Privileges of Church of England with respect to Charities.

[C. T. Act, 1853.]　46. Nothing herein contained shall diminish or detract from any Right or Privilege which by any Rule or Practice of the Court of Chancery, or by the Construction of Law, now subsists for the Preference or the exclusive or special Benefit of the Church of England, or the Members of the same Church, in settling any Scheme for the Regulation of any Charity, or in the Appointment or Removal of Trustees, or generally in the Application or Management of any Charity.

Continuance of powers transferred to Charity Commissioners.

[Endowed Schools Act, 1874 (37 & 38 Vict. c. 87.).]　6. The powers of making Schemes under the Endowed Schools Acts as amended by this Act shall continue in force for a period of five years from the said thirty-first day of December one thousand eight hundred and seventy-four;‡ and during the continuance of such powers any court or judge shall not, with respect to any endowed school or educational endowment which can be dealt with by a scheme under this Act and the Endowed Schools Acts, or any of such Acts, make any scheme or appoint any new trustees without the consent of the Committee of Council on Education.

---

* *Repealed by the Statute Law Revision Act,* 1892 (55 & 56 *Vict. c.* 19.).]
[† *Since* 1856 *the Clerk of a County Court has been called the Registrar of the Court. See County Courts Act,* 1856, *sect.* 8 (19 & 20 *Vict. c.* 108.).]
[‡ *These powers were continued up to* 31 *March* 1898 *by sect.* 1, *sub-sect.* 2, *of Expiring Laws Continuance Act,* 1896, (59 & 60 *Vict. c.* 39.).]

[C. T. Act, 1860.] 11. The Jurisdiction vested by the Charitable Trusts Act, 1853, in the *District Courts of Bankruptcy and** County Courts, over Charities not possessing a larger gross yearly income than Thirty Pounds, shall be exerciseable by the said Courts respectively for the like Purposes and under the like Provisions over Charities of which the gross yearly Income for the Time being, to be calculated in Manner aforesaid,† shall not exceed Fifty Pounds, in the same Manner as if the last-mentioned Limit to the Jurisdiction of the said Courts had been fixed by the said former Act.

Jurisdiction of the District Courts of Bankruptcy and County Courts enlarged.

[C. T. Act, 1853.] 33. *The Jurisdiction hereby created and conferred on the County Courts with respect to any Charity shall not be exercised by any Deputy or other Person who may for the time being be appointed to sit and shall be sitting for any such Judge.‡*

Deputy sitting for County Court Judge not to exercise Jurisdiction.

[C. T. Act, 1853.] 34. Where two or more *District Courts of Bankruptcy or*§ County Courts shall concurrently have Jurisdiction under this Act with respect to any Charity, it shall be lawful for the said Board to order to which of such Courts any Application with respect to such Charity shall be made; and every such Order shall be conclusive as to the Jurisdiction with respect to the Application referred to in such Order.

Where two or more Courts have concurrent Jurisdiction, Board to direct to which Court Applications shall be made.

[C. T. Act, 1853.] 35. It shall be lawful for the said Board to direct that any Application as to any Charity within the Jurisdiction of any *District Court of Bankruptcy or* § County Court shall be made before a Judge of the Court of Chancery, or as to any Charity within the Jurisdiction of the Court of Chancery of the County Palatine of Lancaster, either before the Chancellor or the Vice Chancellor of the same County Palatine, or before a Judge of the High Court of Chancery, according to the Provisions herein contained applicable to a Charity the gross annual Income whereof exceeds Thirty Pounds, and in such Case such Application shall be made and may be heard and determined accordingly, in like Manner as if the gross annual Income of such Charity exceeded Thirty Pounds ; ‖ and upon the Production of the Order or Certificate containing such Direction, or of a Copy thereof, the Application with respect to which such Order or Certificate shall have been made shall not be entertained or proceeded with by such *District or*§ County Court.

Board may direct Cases within the Jurisdiction of a District or County Court to be taken before a Judge of the Court of Chancery in the first instance.

[C. T. Act, 1853.] 44. For the Purposes of determining the Jurisdiction under this Act with respect to any Charity, ... it shall be lawful for the said Board to declare, according to such Judgment as they may be able to form upon the Returns or Statements before them in relation to any Charity, whether the gross annual Income for the Time being of such Charity does or does not exceed Thirty ¶ Pounds . . . . (as the Case may require,) and a Statement in any Certificate or Order of the said Board that according to such Judgment as aforesaid the gross yearly Income of any Charity does or does not exceed Thirty ● Pounds . . . . shall be sufficient Evidence of the Amount of the gross annual Income of such Charity, for the Purpose of determining such Jurisdiction . . . . as aforesaid ; and any Certificate or Order made by the said Board under this Act, authorizing any Proceeding or Application concerning any Charity to be taken or made to any *District Court of Bankruptcy or*§ County Court . . . . shall state that the gross annual Income for the Time being of such Charity does not exceed Thirty ¶ Pounds.

Statement in Certificate of Board of the Amount of Income of any Charity to be sufficient Evidence for determining the Jurisdiction or Proceedings under this Act.

[* *Repealed by the Statute Law Revision Act, 1875 (38 & 39 Vict. c. 66.)*
[† *See Charitable Trusts Act, 1860, sect. 4 (p. 75).*]
[‡ *Repealed by the Statute Law Revision Act, 1875 38 & 39 Vict. c. 66. By the County Courts Act, 1888, sect. 18 (51 & 52 Vict. c. 13.), a deputy Jud has all the powers, &c. of the Judge for whom he is acting.*]
[§ *Repealed by the Statute Law Revision Act, 1892 (55 & 56 Vict. c. 19.).*]
[‖ *As to this procedure, see p. 61.*]
[¶ *Now "Fifty," so far as regards the jurisdiction of the County Courts. See sect. 11 of*
C. T. Act, 1860, supra.]

Proviso as to particular Endowments. Provided always, that where any Charity, or the Trustees thereof, in addition to the principal Endowment for its general Objects and Purposes, shall be possessed of or entitled to any other Endowment for any particular or special Object or Purpose arising out of or in its Nature or Application connected with the general Objects or Purposes of such Charity, it shall be lawful for the said Board, having regard to the Circumstances of each such Case, and to the Object and Extent of the proposed Application and Litigation, to determine whether such Endowment for such particular or special Object or Purpose should, for the Purposes of Jurisdiction and Proceedings under this Act, be considered and treated as forming Part of the general Endowment of the Charity, or as a separate or independent Charity, and such Board shall frame their Certificate or Order accordingly.

[This section is printed in full at p. 63.]

By whom Applications may be made. **[C. T. Act, 1853.] 43.** Every application to any Judge or Court under the Jurisdiction created or conferred by any of the Provisions of this Act, may be made by Her Majesty's Attorney General, or, subject to the Provisions aforesaid, by all or any One or more of the Trustees or Persons administering or claiming to administer, or interested in, the Charity which shall be the Subject of such Application, or any Two or more Inhabitants of any Parish or Place within which the Charity is administered or applicable; . . .

[This section is printed in full in Appendix, No. 1, p. 74.]

Notice to be published of Application for Schemes or Appointment or Removal of Trustees under this Act. **[C. T. Act, 1853.] 42.** Before any Application shall be made . . . . to any *District Court of Bankruptcy or** County Court, under any of the Provisions herein contained for the Establishment or Alteration of a Scheme or the Appointment or Removal of any Trustees or Trustee, Notice in Writing of such intended Application shall be given in such Form and Manner as the said Board shall have directed; and if the Order be that such Notice be affixed to or near the Door of any Parish or District Church, the Incumbent and Churchwardens of such Parish or District are hereby respectively required to allow such Notice to be affixed and to remain so affixed during such Period, not less than Fifteen Days, as the said Board shall have ordered; and in any Case in which the Order shall be that such Notice shall be affixed to any Place, Evidence that the same has been so affixed shall be deemed and taken as primâ facie Evidence that it has remained affixed during the Period prescribed by the Board.

[This section is printed in full in Appendix, No. 1, p. 74.]

No Order of District or County Court for the Appointment or Removal of Trustees or Approval of a Scheme to be valid unless confirmed by Board. **[C. T. Act, 1853.] 36.** Whenever any Order or Decision is made by any *District Court of Bankruptcy or** County Court for the Appointment or Removal of any Trustee of any Charity, or approving of any Scheme for regulating or directing the Administration of any Charity, or the Estate, Funds, Property, or Income thereof, a Copy of every such Order or Decision shall immediately upon the making thereof be delivered or transmitted *by the Deputy Registrar of such District Court or** by the Clerk† of the County Court, *as the Case may be,** together with all requisite Particulars, to the said Board, for the Purpose of being considered by them; and no such Order or Decision shall be valid or effectual until the same shall have been approved by the said Board, such approval to be testified by a Certificate in Writing, signed by the Secretary of the said Board,‡ and no such Approval shall issue from the said Board until One Calendar Month shall have elapsed after the Receipts by the Board of such Copy and Particulars.

Board, if dissatisfied with the **[C. T. Act, 1853.] 37.** In case any such Order or Decision as last aforesaid of any *District Court of Bankruptcy or** County Court shall not be

---

[* *Repealed by the Statute Law Revision Act*, 1892 (55 & 56 Vict. c. 19.).]
[† *Now "the Registrar." See footnote* † *on p. 66.*]
[‡ *But see now Charitable Trusts Amendment Act*, 1855, *sect.* 4 (*p.* 16), *and Charitable Trusts Act*, 1887, *sect.* 3 (*p.* 16).]

approved by the said Board, it shall be lawful for such Board to remit the same for Reconsideration and Decision by such *District or** County Court, with such Remarks and Recommendations thereon (if any) as shall seem fit and expedient to such Board, or, in the Discretion of the Board, to order, and direct that the Subject Matter to which such Order or Decision relates, together with such Order or Decision, shall be submitted to the Consideration and Decision of a Judge of the Court of Chancery, and in such last-mentioned Case no further Proceedings shall be had or taken in the *District or** County Court with respect to the Matter in question ; and in case the Order or Decision of the *District or** County Court, on the Reconsideration of any Order or Decision so remitted for Reconsideration, be disapproved as aforesaid by the said Board, such Board shall refer such Orders and Decisions, and the Subject Matter thereof, to a Judge of the Court of Chancery, or, as to any Charity within the Jurisdiction of the Court of Chancery of the County Palatine of Lancaster, either to the Chancellor or the Vice Chancellor of the same County Palatine, or to a Judge of the High Court of Chancery ; and where any Order or Decision is referred to a Judge of the Court of Chancery, or of the Court of Chancery of the said County Palatine of Lancaster, under this Provision, such Judge shall have and exercise all such Jurisdiction, Power, and Authority in relation thereto as in the Case of a Charity the gross annual Income whereof exceeds Thirty Pounds,† and may make such Order in relation to the Matter of such Order or Decision as to him may seem proper.

(margin: Order of District or CountyCourt may remit the Case for Reconsideration, or may transfer the Matter to a Judge of the Court of Chancery.)

[C. T. Act, 1853.] 38. Subject to any Orders to be made by the Lord Chancellor as herein-after mentioned, and to the other Provisions of this Act, all Proceedings to be taken in any *District Court of Bankruptcy or** County Court, and all Orders and Directions to be made or given by any such *District Court or** County Court by virtue of the Jurisdiction hereby created and conferred on such Court, shall respectively be subject to the same Rules and Regulations, and have the same Effect, and be registered, enforced, and executed in the same Manner, as the other Proceedings, Orders, Judgments, and Directions of the same Court under its ordinary Jurisdiction, and it shall be lawful *for any such District Court or** for any County Court, with the Consent of the Board, to rescind or vary any Order which shall have been previously made by such Court, without Prejudice to any Act or Matter in the meantime done under such Order ; and for executing and putting in force any Order to be made by any County Court under this Act, every Judge of any such Court shall and may have and exercise all such Powers *as by the Act of the Session holden in the Ninth and Tenth Years of Her Majesty, Chapter Ninety-five,‡* are given for enforcing the Payment of any Debt, Damages, or Costs under the said Act.

(margin: How Orders of District or County Court under this Act to be enforced.)

[C. T. Act, 1853.] 45. The Lord Chancellor shall make such Orders for regulating Proceedings by and before the Judges of *District Courts of Bankruptcy and** County Courts under this Act, and for fixing and determining the Fees to be taken in respect of such Proceedings, as he may see fit ; and, subject to such Orders, such Judges may regulate the Proceedings before them respectively so as to render them as summary and inexpensive as conveniently may be.

(margin: Lord Chancellor to make Orders for regulating Proceedings before District and County Courts Judges to regulate Proceedings.)

[C. T. Act, 1853.] 39. Where any Person authorized to make any Application under this Act, (other than Her Majesty's Attorney General acting ex-officio,) or any other Person who may have been made a Party to any Proceeding upon any Application under this Act, is aggrieved by or dissatisfied with any Order made by any *District Court of Bankruptcy or** County Court upon any such Application, or any Proceeding thereon, he may, within One Calendar Month after the making of such Order, give

(margin: Appeal.)

[* *Repealed by the Statute Law Revision Act,* 1892 (55 & 56 *Vict. c.* 19).]
[† *As to this procedure, see ante,* p. 61.]
[‡ *For the Act here cited, read ' County Courts Act,* 1888 ;" *see sect.* 188, *sub-sect.* 3, *of this latter Act* (51 & 52 *Vict. c.* 43).]

I 3

Notice in Writing to the said Court, and also to the said Board, that he is desirous to appeal against the same; and if the said Board think it reasonable and proper that such Appeal should be entertained, and give a Certificate to that Effect, such *District or** County Court shall suspend any Proceedings upon the Order appealed against during such Time as the Circumstances may require; and the said Board, if they so think fit, may require the Person giving any such Notice of Appeal to become bound with Two sufficient Sureties, to be approved *by the Deputy Registrar of such District Court, or** by the Clerk of the County Court,† *as the Case may be,** to the Treasurers of the said Courts respectively, or such other Person as the said Board may see fit, in such Sum as to the said Board shall seem reasonable, to pay such Costs of the Proceedings on the Appeal as shall be ordered to be paid by such Appellant, and also (if the said Board so think fit) to indemnify the Charity against the Costs and Expenses of or attending such Appeal; and every Bond executed under this Provision shall be exempt from Stamp Duty: Provided always, that it shall be lawful for Her Majesty's Attorney General, (acting ex-officio,) at any Time within Three Calendar Months after *the making of any Order by a *District Court or** County Court under this Act, to lodge and commence and prosecute an Appeal against such Order, without giving any such Notice or becoming bound as aforesaid, and every such last-mentioned Appeal shall thereupon be allowed by the Order of such *District or** County Court, and shall have such other Effect as any other Appeal under this Act.

Proceedings on Appeal.   [C. T. Act, 1853.] **40.** Where any Order allowing an Appeal has been made as aforesaid, the Person thereby allowed to appeal shall within Three Calendar Months present a Petition to the Court of Chancery, setting forth the Order appealed against, and the Order allowing such Appeal, and praying such Relief as the Case may require; and upon the hearing of such Petition the Court may confirm, vary, or reverse the Order appealed against, or may remit such Order to the *District Court of Bankruptcy or** County Court by which the same was made, with or without any Declaration or Directions of the Court of Chancery in relation thereto, or may proceed in relation to the Charity to which such Order relates as in the Case of an Application under this Act to a Judge of the Court of Chancery at Chambers, and any Judge of such Court sitting at Chambers or in open Court may make or give any such Orders or Directions in relation to the Matter of such Order as he may see fit, or the Court may make such other Order in relation to the Matter of any such Appeal as to the Court may seem just, and as might be made in the Case of a Suit regularly instituted, or a Petition, as the Case may require; and in case the Party allowed to appeal do not within Three Calendar Months present such Petition of Appeal, the Order against which such Appeal was **Bond to prosecute Appeal may be put in Suit.**   allowed shall be final; and in case any Costs adjudged on any such Appeal to be paid by the Party allowed to appeal be not paid, such Bond as aforesaid may be put in Suit, and the Money to be recovered on every such Bond shall be applied to indemnify the Charity Estate or the Person damnified, or otherwise in such Manner as the Justice of the Case may require, and the Court or Judge by whom such Appeal may have been heard shall think fit.

(*h.*) *RECOVERY, UNDER WARRANT OF JUSTICES, OF POSSESSION OF CHARITY PROPERTY HELD OVER BY OFFICER OR ANY RECIPIENT OF CHARITY.*

Power for Magistrates to give Possession of   [C. T. Act, 1860.] **13.** Where any School Master or Mistress or other Officer, or any Recipient of the Benefit of a Charity, being in possession by virtue of his or her Office, or as such Recipient, of any House, Buildings, Land,

---

[* *Repealed by the Statute Law Revision Act,* 1892 (55 & 56 *Vict. c.* 19.).]
[† *Now "the Registrar." *See footnote* ‡ *on* p. 66.]

or Property of the Charity, shall have been removed from or shall cease to hold such his or her Office, or his or her Place as such Recipient, but he or she, or any Person claiming under him or her, shall refuse or neglect to relinquish the Possession of such House, Buildings, Land, or Property within One Calendar Month next thereafter, to his or her Successor, or to the Trustees or Persons acting in the Administration of the Charity, or as they shall direct, it shall be lawful for any Two or more Justices of the Peace acting for the District, Division, or Place in which such House, Buildings, Land, or Property shall be situate, in Petty Sessions assembled, and they are hereby required, on the Complaint of the said Trustees or Administrators, and on the Production of an Order of the said Board certifying such School Master or Mistress or other Officer or Recipient to have been duly removed from or to have ceased to hold his or her Office or Place, (which Order under the Seal of the said Commissioners shall be conclusive Evidence of the Facts thereby certified, and of the Jurisdiction of the said Commissioners to make such Order for all the Purposes of this Enactment and shall afford a complete Indemnity to all persons acting thereunder,) to issue a Warrant under the Hands and Seals of such Justices to any Constables or Peace Officers of the same District, Division, or Place, commanding them, within a Period to be thereby appointed, not being less than Ten or more than Twenty-one clear Days thereafter, to enter into the Premises, and deliver Possession thereof to the said Trustees or Administrators, or their Nominee or Agent, and to remove therefrom such former School Master or Mistress, or other Officer or Recipient, and all Persons claiming in his or her Right, as fully and effectually, and subject to the same Provisions, as nearly as the Case will permit, as Justices of the Peace are empowered to give Possession of any Properties to the Landlord or his Agent upon the Determination of the Tenancy thereof, under an Act passed in the First and Second Years of the Reign of Her Majesty, Chapter Seventy-four, for facilitating the Recovery of Possession of Tenements after the Determination of the Tenancy.

[Marginal note: School Buildings and Property held over by Officers or Recipients of Charities.]

XII.—Provisions as to Repeals.

[C. T. Act, 1855.] 1. "The Charitable Trusts Act, 1853," herein-after called "the principal Act," and this Act, shall be construed together as One Act, and any Provisions of the principal Act inconsistent with this Act are hereby repealed.

[Marginal note: 16 & 17 Vict. c. 137, and this Act to be construed together.]

[C. T. Act, 1855.] 2. *So much of the principal Act (Section 11.) as provides that after the Thirty-first Day of March One thousand eight hundred and fifty-seven an annual Salary shall be paid to One only of the Commissioners besides the Chief Commissioner is hereby repealed.**

[Marginal note: Provision as to the Salary of One of the Commissioners repealed.]

[C. T. Act, 1855.] 30. *So much of Section Twenty-one of the principal Act as requires a compulsory Provision to be inserted in every Mortgage for the Payment of the Principal Money borrowed by annual Instalments, and for the Redemption and Reconveyance of the mortgaged Estates within the Period of not more than Thirty Years, is hereby repealed ;** . .*

[Marginal note: Sinking Fund to be provided for paying off Mortgages in Lieu of Provision in Mortgage Deeds.]

[*This section is printed in full at p. 27.*]

[C. T. Act, 1855.] 41. Section Twenty-seven of "The Charitable Trusts Act, 1853,"† shall be construed and operate as if the Words " and " the Trustees of the Charity shall be legally authorized to purchase and " hold such land " had been omitted therefrom ; . . . . .

[Marginal note: Construction of Sect. 27, of 16 & 17 Vict. c. 137.]

[*This section is printed in full at p. 25.*]

[* *Repealed by the Statute Law Revision Act,* 1875 (38 & 39 Vict. c. 66).]   [† p. 25.]

I 4

Construction of Sects. 55 and 59 of 16 & 17 Vict. c. 137.

[C. T. Act, 1855.] **43.** The Fifty-fifth* and Fifty-ninth† Sections of the principal Act shall be construed and operate as if the Words "The Office of the Board" had been inserted therein in the Place of the Words "the Office in London of the Registrar of County Courts Judgments."

Amendment of Sect. 61. of 16 & 17 Vict. c. 137. and other Provision made as to the Annual Returns of Accounts by Trustees of Charities.

[C. T. Act, 1855.] **44.** *Section Sixty-one‡ of " The Charitable Trusts Act, 1853," except so much thereof as enacts that the Trustees or Persons acting in the administration of every Charity shall, in Books to be kept by them for that Purpose, regularly enter or cause to be entered full and true Accounts of all Money received and paid respectively on account of such Charity, shall be repealed as to all Accounts which such Trustees or Administrators shall not have been bound to render before the passing of this Act ;* §   . . .

[This section is printed in full at p. 21.]

The Charitable Trusts Acts to be construed with this Act.

[C. T. Act, 1860.] **1.** "The Charitable Trusts Act, 1853," and "The Charitable Trusts Amendment Act, 1855," and this Act, shall be construed together as One Act, and any Provisions of the said former Acts inconsistent with this Act are hereby repealed.

Repeal.

[C. T. Act, 1869.] **17.** ‖*The enactments described in the schedule to this Act are hereby repealed ; provided that,*

(1.) *This repeal shall not affect anything already done and suffered, or any right acquired or order made, under such enactments :*

(2.) *Any proceedings already commenced under the enactments hereby repealed shall be proceeded with in the same manner as if this repeal had not been made.*

‖ *SCHEDULE.*

Date.	Title.	
16 & 17 Vict. c. 137. -	An Act for the better administration of Charitable Trusts - - -	In part ; namely, section sixty-three.
23 & 24 Vict. c. 136. -	An Act to amend the law relating to the administration of Endowed Charities. -	In part ; namely, section sixteen.

Repeal.

[C. T. Act, 1887.] **6.** The Acts specified in the Second Schedule to this Act are hereby repealed to the extent in the third column of that schedule mentioned : Provided that

(*a*) this repeal shall not affect anything already done or suffered, or the tenure, salary, or power of any officer holding office at the passing of this Act ;

(*b*) this repeal, so far as regards the official trustees of charitable funds, shall take effect on the date on which regulations under this Act in relation to such trustees come into operation.¶

[* p. 52.]   [† p. 53.]   [‡ p. 20.]
[§ *Repealed by the Statute Law Revision Act, 1875 (38 & 39 Vict. c. 66.).*]
[‖ *Repealed by the Statute Law Revision Act, 1883 (46 & 47 Vict. c. 39.).*]
[¶ *1st April 1889.*]

SECOND SCHEDULE.

ENACTMENTS REPEALED.

Session and Chapter.	Title of Act.	Part repealed.
16 & 17 Vict. c. 137. -	The Charitable Trusts Act, 1853	So much of section one as relates to the inspectors; section four, section fifty-one down to " charitable funds and " inclusive, and section fifty-two down to the words " each separate charity and " inclusive.
18 & 19 Vict. c. 124. -	The Charitable Trusts Amendment Act, 1855.	Section three; in section four the words " or in his absence, of the chief clerk "; in section five the words " or in his absence, of the chief clerk "; section seventeen; in section eighteen the word " present," and the words " to be so appointed "; section twenty, from the words " and the secretary " inclusive to end of section; section twenty-four, from " and the said trustees " inclusive to end of section.
23 & 24 Vict. c. 136. -	The Charitable Trusts Act, 1860	In section seventeen the words " appointed under or in pursuance of " the first or secondly recited Act."

APPENDIX No. 1.

CONTAINING IN FULL CERTAIN SECTIONS OF THE CHARITABLE TRUSTS ACTS, THE SEVERAL PARTS OF WHICH ARE PRINTED SEPARATELY IN THE TEXT.

No Chancery Judge, or District or County Court, in Proceedings under this Act to try Titles, &c.

[C. T. Act, 1853.] **41.** Provided always, That no Judge of the Court of Chancery nor any *District Court of Bankruptcy or* County Court, shall upon any Proceedings under this Act have Jurisdiction to try or determine the Title at Law or in Equity to any Real or Personal Property, or any Term or Interest therein, as between any Charity, or the Trustee thereof, and any Person holding or claiming such Real or Personal Property, Term, or Interest adversely to such Charity, or to try or determine any Question as to the existence or Extent of any Charge or Trust.

Notice to be published of Application for Schemes or Appointment or Removal of Trustees under this Act.

[C. T. Act, 1853.] **42.** Before any Application shall be made to any Judge of the Court of Chancery, or to any *District Court of Bankruptcy or* County Court, under any of the Provisions herein contained for the Establishment or Alteration of a Scheme or the Appointment or Removal of any Trustees or Trustee, Notice in Writing of such intended Application shall be given in such Form and Manner as the said Board shall have directed ; and if the Order be that such Notice be affixed to or near the Door of any Parish or District Church, the Incumbent and Churchwardens of such Parish or District are hereby respectively required to allow such Notice to be affixed and to remain so affixed during such Period, not less than Fifteen Days, as the said Board shall have ordered ; and in any Case in which the Order shall be that such Notice shall be affixed to any Place, Evidence that the same has been so affixed shall be deemed and taken as primâ facie Evidence that it has remained affixed during the Period prescribed by the Board.

By whom Applications may be made.

Attorney General may Petition under 52 G. 3. c. 101.

[C. T. Act, 1853.] **43.** Every Application to any Judge or Court under the Jurisdiction created or conferred by any of the Provisions of this Act, may be made by Her Majesty's Attorney General, or, subject to the Provisions aforesaid, by all or any One or more of the Trustees or Persons administering or claiming to administer, or interested in, the Charity which shall be the Subject of such Application, or any Two or more Inhabitants of any Parish or Place within which the Charity is administered or applicable ; and it shall be lawful for Her Majesty's Attorney General for the Time being, acting ex officio, to make application by Petition to the Court of Chancery with respect to any Charity under the Provisions of the Act passed in the Fifty-second Year of King George the Third, Chapter One hundred and one, or under the Provisions of any Act or Acts passed or to be passed authorizing the Application to the same Court by Petition according to the Provisions of the said Act.

Judge may order Trustees, &c. holding Stock, &c. belonging to a Charity subject to his Jurisdiction to transfer same to Official Trustees.

[C. T. Act, 1853.] **51.** *The Secretary for the Time being of the said Board, and such other public Officer or Officers as the Lord Chancellor shall appoint, shall be official Trustees of Charitable Funds, and* where Trustees or other Persons having in their Names, or in the Name of any deceased Person of whom they are Representatives, in the Books of the Bank of England, or of the East India or South Sea Company, or of any other public Company, any Annuities, Stock or Shares, or holding any Government or Parliamentary or other Securities in trust for any Charity, shall be desirous to transfer or deposit the same to or with the said official Trustees in trust for such Charity, or where any Persons shall be desirous of transferring or depositing as aforesaid any Annuities, Stocks, Shares, or Securities, for discharging any Legacy or Charge given or made to or for the Benefit of any Charity, or where it shall appear to the Court of Chancery, or to any Judge of such Court, or of any *District Court of Bankruptcy,* or County Court having Jurisdiction under this Act, that any Annuities, Stock, Shares, or Securities, held in trust for any Charity ought, for the Purpose of Security or convenient Administration, to be transferred or deposited as aforesaid, it shall be lawful for such Court or Judge to order the Transfer or Deposit of such Annuities, Stock, Shares, or Securities to or with such official Trustees.

Expenses of Exchanges and Partitions, and determining Application of Charges.

[C. T. Act, 1855.] **34.** The Expenses incident to the Application for and procuring of any such Order of Exchange or Partition, or Order determining the Land charged with any Rent, Annuity, or Periodical Payment, shall be paid by the Trustees or Administrators of the Charity, or by the other Parties to such Transactions, or by both, as the Board may direct.

Board may direct Official Trustees to convey Lands, &c.

[C. T. Act, 1855.] **37.** It shall be lawful for the Board to authorize or order and direct the Official Trustee of Charity Lands and the Official Trustees of Charitable Funds respectively to convey Lands, and to assign, transfer, and pay over Stocks, Funds, Monies, and Securities, as the Board shall think expedient.

[C. T. Act, 1860.] 2. The Board of Charity Commissioners for England and Wales, subject to the Restrictions and Rights of Appeal herein-after provided, shall have Power from Time to Time, upon the Application of any Person or Persons who, under the Forty-third Section of "The Charitable Trusts Act, 1853," might be authorized to apply to any Judge or Court for the like Purposes, to make such effectual Orders as may now be made by any Judge of the Court of Chancery sitting at Chambers, or by any County Court or District Court of Bankruptcy, for the Appointment or Removal of Trustees of any Charity, or for the Removal of any School Master or Mistress or other Officer thereof, or for or relating to the Assurance, Transfer, Payment, or vesting of any Real or Personal Estate belonging thereto, or entitling the Official Trustees of Charitable Funds, or any other Trustees, to call for a Transfer of and to transfer any Stock belonging to such Estate, or for the Establishment of any Scheme for the Administration of any such Charity.

Certain administrative Powers to be exercisable by the Charity Commissioners.

[C. T. Act, 1860.] 4. The said Board shall not make any Order, under the Jurisdiction vested in them by this Act, with respect to any Charity of which the gross annual Income, exclusively of the yearly Value of any Buildings or Land used wholly for the Purposes thereof, and not yielding any pecuniary Income, shall amount to Fifty Pounds or upwards, except upon the Application of the Trustees or Persons acting in the Administration of the Charity, or a Majority of them, to be made to the said Board in Writing under their Hands if they shall be unincorporated, or under their Common Seal if they shall be incorporated, and the Board shall not make any Order removing any Trustee on the Ground only of his Religious Belief.

The Powers to be exercisable over no Charities of which the gross Income shall exceed 50l. without Application of Trustees.

[C. T. Act, 1860.] 6. No Order appointing or removing a Trustee, or establishing a Scheme for the Administration of any Charity, shall be made by the said Board before the Expiration of One Calendar Month after public Notice of the Proposal to make such Order shall have been given, as they may consider most expedient and effectual for ensuring the Publicity thereof, in each Parish or District in which the Charity, if of a local Character, shall be applicable, or among all Persons interested therein; and no Order removing a Trustee or School Master or Mistress or other Officer of a Charity who shall have any known Place of Residence in Great Britain or Ireland, and who shall not be consenting to be discharged, shall be made before the Expiration of One Calendar Month after Notice of the Proposal to make such Order shall have also been delivered to him or her, or sent by the Post or otherwise to such his or her Place of Residence, and until after sufficient Hearing of the Matter before the said Board, or some Member thereof, or One of their Inspectors; and every Notice hereby required shall contain (so far as conveniently may be) sufficient Particulars of the Objects of the proposed Order, and shall prescribe a reasonable Time within which any Objections thereto or Suggestions thereon may be made or transmitted to the Board; and the said Board shall receive and consider all such Objections and Suggestions, and may withhold, suspend, or modify their proposed Order, as they shall thereupon, or in the Result of further Inquiry, or otherwise, think expedient.

Notices to be given of certain Orders, and Objections or Suggestions to be received.

[C. T. Act, 1860.] 8. The Attorney General, or any Person authorized by him or by the said Board, in the Case of any Charity, whatever may be the yearly Income of its Endowments, and any Trustee or Person acting in the Administration of or interested in any Charity of which the gross yearly Income to be calculated in manner aforesaid shall exceed Fifty Pounds, or any Two Inhabitants of any Parish or District in which the same shall be specially applicable, may, within Three Calendar Months next after the definitive Publication of any Order of the said Board appointing or removing a Trustee or Trustees, or for or relating to the Assurance, Transfer, Payment, or vesting of any Real or Personal Estate, or establishing a Scheme for the Administration of the Charity, present a Petition to the High Court of Chancery in a summary Way, appealing against such Order, and praying such Relief as the Case may require; and any Schoolmaster or Schoolmistress or other Officer removed by the Order of the Board, without the Concurrence of the Trustees or Persons acting in the Administration of the Charity, or a Majority of them, and without the Approval of a Special Visitor, if any, of the Charity, may, within Two Calendar Months (next after his or her Removal), appeal in like Manner against the Order of Removal; and the Court, upon or before the Hearing of any such Petition of Appeal as aforesaid or at any Stage of the Proceedings, may require, if it shall think fit, from the said Board, their Reasons for making the Order appealed against, or for any Part of such Order, and may remit the same to the Board for Reconsideration, with or without any Declaration in relation thereto, or may make any substitutive or other Order in relation to the Matter of the Appeal, as it shall think just; and the Court may make any Order respecting the Costs, Charges, or Expenses incident to the Appeal, and may also, before hearing or proceeding with the same, require from any Appellant, other than the Attorney General, proper Security for such Costs, Charges, and Expenses as may be eventually payable by him; but no such Petition of Appeal shall be presented by any Person, other than the Attorney General, before the expiration of Twenty-one Days after written Notice, under the Hand of such

Power to appeal against Orders of Board.

Appellant, of his or her Intention to present such Petition, shall have been delivered to the said Board at their Office.

[**C. T. Act, 1862.**] Whereas by the Acts relating to the Charity Commissioners for England and Wales, Authority has been given to the Commissioners to make Orders for various Purposes in Charity Cases upon summary Application, and particularly in relation to the Appointment and Removal of Trustees, and the Sale, Exchange, Leasing, and Improvement of the Property of Charities: And whereas in various Private Acts of Parliament and Decrees and Orders of the High Court of Chancery relating to Charities such Powers and Authorities are often given or reserved, with Directions that the same shall be exercised by the said Court, or with its Sanction or Approbation, and Doubts are entertained whether in such Cases the Authority given to the Charity Commissioners can be validly exercised: Be it therefore enacted and declared *by the Queen's most Excellent Majesty, by and with the advice and consent of the Lords Spiritual and Temporal, and Commons, in this present Parliament assembled, and by the authority of the same* as follows:

No Provision in any Act of Parliament, or Decree relating to any Charity under any Order of the Court of Chancery, to exclude any Jurisdiction which might otherwise be exercised by the Charity Commissioners.

1. No Provision contained in any such Act of Parliament or Decree or Order as aforesaid for the Appointment or Removal of Trustees of any Charity, or for or relating to the Sale, Exchange, Leasing, Disposal, or Improvement of any Property, by or under the Order or with the Approval of the Court of Chancery, shall (in the Absence of any express Direction to the contrary, to be contained in any future Act of Parliament, Order, or Decree,) exclude or impair any Jurisdiction or Authority which might otherwise be properly exercised for the like Purposes by the Charity Commissioners for England and Wales.

[**C. T. Act, 1887.**] **4.**—(1.) From and after the date fixed by a regulation under this section, such officers of the Board as the Board with the approval of the Treasury from time to time appoint shall, in lieu of the persons mentioned in the Charitable Trusts Amendment Act, 1855, be the official trustees of charitable funds:

Amendment of Charitable Trusts Acts as to official trustees of charitable funds.

Provided that any inspector or officer of the Board, who at the passing of this Act is official trustee of charitable funds, and is not, after the passing of this Act, appointed to be official trustee, shall, while he continues to hold his inspectorship or office, receive not less salary than he received while official trustee.

(2.) From and after the said date, notwithstanding anything in the Charitable Trusts Acts, 1853 to 1869, the Treasury may, by regulations to be made or approved by them, from time to time prescribe:

   (*a*) the accounts to be kept by the said official trustees and the mode in which and the persons by whom such accounts and the banking accounts, and any other accounts required by the Charitable Trusts Acts, 1853 to 1869, to be kept by or on behalf of the official trustees of charitable funds, are to be kept;

   (*b*) the mode in which orders authorised by law for the payment of any money to or by the said official trustees or held upon their banking account, or for the transfer of any stock or securities to or by the said official trustees, are to be signed, authenticated, and carried into effect; and

   (*c*) the mode in which the business of the said official trustees generally is to be conducted:

Provided that separate accounts shall continue to be kept for each charity.

(3.) The accounts of the said official trustees shall be audited by such person and in accordance with such regulations as the Treasury from time to time appoint or prescribe.

(4.) A regulation under this section, or any order made under any such regulation, shall be a complete indemnity to the Governor and Company of the Bank of England, and all companies and persons, for any act done pursuant to such regulation or order, and the said Governor and Company, and other companies and persons, shall conform to such regulation or order.

APPENDIX No. 2.

THE ENDOWED SCHOOLS ACT, 1874 (37 & 38 VICT. C. 87.).

2. Her Majesty *and her successors* may at any time *after the passing of this Act*, by warrant under her sign manual, from time to time appoint any number of persons not exceeding two to be paid Charity Commissioners for England and Wales and a person to be Secretary in addition to the three paid Charity Commissioners and Secretary capable of being appointed under the Charitable Trusts Acts, 1853 to 1869. The two additional Commissioners and additional Secretary appointed in pursuance of this Act shall hold office during Her Majesty's pleasure, and their salaries shall, unless otherwise directed by Parliament, cease to be paid after the expiration of five years from the said thirty-first day of December one thousand eight hundred and seventy-four.

Save as in this section mentioned, the additional Commissioners shall have the same powers, perform the same duties, and stand in all respects in the same position as the other paid Charity Commissioners with the exception of the Chief Commissioner.

The *Commissioners of Her Majesty's* Treasury may allow the Charity Commissioners to employ such number of assistant commissioners, officers, and clerks as the *Commissioners of Her Majesty's* Treasury may think necessary for the purpose of enabling the said Charity Commissioners to perform the additional duties imposed upon them by this Act.

Power to add to Charity Commissioners.

INDEX TO SECTIONS OF THE CHARITABLE TRUSTS ACTS, 1853 to 1894.

GENERAL INDEX.

Subject.	Page.